The Silent Pool

AND OTHER STORIES

R. E. LOTEN

CASTLE PRIORY PRESS

First published in Great Britain in 2023 by Castle Priory Press, Brightlingsea

978-1-7398867-7-6

Copyright © R.E. Loten, 2023

The moral right of the author has been asserted.

All characters and events in this publication, other than those in the public domain, are fictitious and any resemblance to real persons, living or dead, is purely coincidental.

All rights reserved. No part of this publication may be reproduced, stored in a retrieval system, or transmitted, in any form, or by any means, without the prior permission in writing of the publisher, nor be otherwise circulated in any form of binding or cover other than that in which it is published and without a similar condition including this condition being imposed on the subsequent purchaser.

Contents

Acknowledgments — vii

1. The Silent Pool — 1
2. Lockdown Love Affair — 6
3. I Am Not Who I Am — 9
4. The Date — 17
5. Spes Mea In Deo* — 23
6. Eagle One Eagle Two — 30
7. The Grave Man — 38
8. The Flight — 45
9. The Railway — 48
10. Through The Glass Darkly — 50
11. A Passing Fancy — 57
12. Under The Hammer — 62
13. Dream A Little Dream Of Me — 66
14. Tweeting Jolene — 73
15. Tarosvan or 'The Legend of Logres' — 75
16. Wait For No Man — 82
17. Who Parents The Parents? — 89
18. Christmas Eve — 92
19. The Yellow Lily — 94
20. The Merry Maidens — 101
21. Archie's Bolero — 108
22. The Few — 117
23. A Steamy Encounter — 120
24. Wyndham's Oak — 123
25. Cake — 126
26. The Garden Of Eden — 128
27. The Injured Queen Of England — 131
28. The Edinburgh Tattoo — 139
29. Coming Home To Cornwall — 145

30. She Who Makes Me Sin	147
About the Author	201
Also by R. E. Loten	203
'Unforgettable'	204
'The Reign Of The Winter King'	217
'Folly'	224

For James

Acknowledgments

My husband was the first person to read many of these stories and without his support, none of them would have been written, as they all came about – one way or another – because of him encouraging me to apply to do a Masters in Creative Writing.

I also have to thank Jane and Dini, who were my fellow Makarelle conspirators and allowed me the freedom to explore the darker side of my imagination. Ultimately, their support and guidance made my writing far better than it otherwise might have been.

In some stories I have taken liberties with the details of actual locations for the purposes of plot.

The Silent Pool

Lily pressed a tissue to her lip, trying to stem the flow of blood. This was it. This time he was going to kill her. She'd never seen him so angry before. It never took much to set him off, but she'd asked for it this evening. She contradicted him in front of his friends, something that was definitely high on the list of things she should never do. Andrew didn't like being told he was wrong and to embarrass him in front of his friends was unforgivable. She hadn't meant to and as soon as the words left her mouth she knew she would pay for them. She just hadn't expected it to be this bad.

Foolishly, she had assumed the punishment would come when they got back to her flat but when he said nothing as they got in the car, she allowed herself to hope that in the pleasant evening that followed her faux pas, he might have forgotten it. After all, he'd continued to pay her compliments and laughed at her jokes during dinner, even putting his arm around her as they sat talking in the living room with his friends. Instead, he was merely biding his time, giving her time to relax before exacting his revenge. He waited until they were on a deserted stretch of road, then stopped the car and yanked her door open.

'Get out!'

Lily obediently unclipped her seatbelt, wondering if he was simply going to abandon her at the side of the road. She was too slow in following his instructions though and his hand shot through the open door and hauled her out of the car by her hair. She whimpered in pain and fear, having learnt any extraneous show of emotion only made him angrier. Her head slammed into the roof of the car and she felt the skin below her eye split.

'Bitch!' He wiped the spit from his lips. 'Feel. Clever. Now?'

Each word was accentuated by a blow across her face and through the haze of pain she was aware of a second stream of blood trickling down her chin.

She shook her head.

'Who wrote *Gone With The Wind*?'

Now she was permitted to speak.

'Margaret Bond.'

Another blow landed.

'I can't hear you. Margaret who?'

'Bond.'

'I knew I was right. Don't mumble in future. And sort yourself out. You're a proper mess. You could at least make an effort to look nice when we see my friends.'

With shaking hands, Lily re-pinned her hair and adjusted her dress. When she'd finished, Andrew gave her a cursory glance.

'It's a bit better, I suppose. Get in the car.'

He closed the door gently and resumed their journey.

'Do you mind if I stay over tonight? I thought we could try that new place for breakfast tomorrow.'

Lily's fingers tightened around her bag. *He's a psychopath.*

No wonder his first wife left him. She saw him clearly for the first time in the three months they'd been dating. His sob story about his wife had been a lie. He wasn't the vulnerable, betrayed, broken man he'd made himself out to be. How had she ever believed him to be? His charm was all on the surface and it had blinded her to his faults, allowed her to believe him when he'd cried and apologised and promised never to hurt her again.

'Of course,' she said brightly. 'Sounds lovely.'

If she was going to act, it had to be fast and it had to be unexpected. She had no doubt there was more planned once they got back to the flat and if he got her inside there'd be no escape. She needed to catch him unawares. Looking out of her window, she realised they were approaching a junction where there was a wooded area in which she might lose him. As he slowed the car to make the right-hand turn onto the A248, Lily unfastened her seatbelt, wrenched the car door open and rolled out onto the road. Ignoring the pain in her shoulder and blessing Andrew's insistence that she wear flat shoes to avoid making him look short, she was off the tarmac and heading for the cover of the nearby woods almost before Andrew had managed to bring the car to a full stop. By the time he recovered from the shock of her escape, parked the car and set off in pursuit, she was plunging into the shelter of the trees. However, she knew his longer legs would catch her up before too long. All she could do was to get as far away as possible then find somewhere to hide and hope for the best.

Drawing in deep shuddering breaths that made her ribs ache, Lily skidded to a halt at the edge of the lake. *Dammit.* She'd forgotten how big The Silent Pool was. If she tried to go around the side there was a good chance Andrew would see her, but it was unthinkable to attempt to swim across it. Andrew was a non-swimmer so she'd be safe from him, but it was dark and she had no desire to leap from one risk of death to another. It was too cloudy for the moon to offer her any help and she didn't trust her ability to find the other bank without it. Fighting off the rising panic, she pushed her way into the bushes and pulled the leaves back into place, hoping her dark dress would camouflage her if Andrew came this way.

With a sinking heart, she heard him crashing through the foliage and willed herself to stay calm.

'I can see you, Lily! You can't outrun me. Just come back to the car and we can talk about this. I'm sorry I lost my temper.'

She held her breath, uncertain how close he was and prayed he was bluffing.

'Sweetheart? I'm sorry. Please wait.'

His voice was nearer now. Lily felt something brush past her hiding place and stifled a gasp, but then Andrew appeared a little way off, his tone altered again.

'Stupid girl. You're trapped. There's nowhere left to run, is there? Unless you're planning to swim for it!'

Lily found a little gap in the leaves. Andrew wasn't looking at her at all. He was staring at a spot at the edge of the lake.

'Why did you run, Lily? I didn't mean to get angry. Forgive me?'

Lily could just make out the dark figure of a woman at the water's edge. Receiving no reply to his question, Andrew tried again.

'Come back to the car, Lily. I won't hurt you again, I promise.'

Still the figure made no denial of her identity. Instead, she turned and began wading out into the dark waters of the lake. With a shout – whether of fear or rage, Lily couldn't tell – Andrew leapt across the remaining distance and strode into the water after her. The woman turned at the sound of splashing and it seemed to Lily, frozen to the spot, that she looked right at her. With an odd half smile, the woman turned and continued her path through the water, Andrew following closely behind her. His grasping fingers reached out to take hold of her arm and then suddenly he disappeared under the surface of the lake. Lily couldn't prevent a squeak of alarm escaping and she waited for a moment, expecting him to rise, spluttering, but there was no sign of him. The Silent Pool was true to its name once more and nothing marred its smooth facade.

Shaken, but unable to stop the wave of relief that washed over her, Lily shouldered her way into the open. Taking her phone out of her bag, she dialled the emergency number.

'Hello? I need to report an accident.'

Once she was assured the police were on their way, her calm demeanour deserted her and shivers racked her body as she wondered how she was going to explain Andrew's disappearance.

'I don't know who you are,' she whispered into the silence, 'But thank-you.'

There was no reply, just a gentle ripple that ran across the water.

Commended in Southport Writers Circle competition, 2021

Lockdown Love Affair

Angie took a last look at the list of people who were working a shift that day and stretched out in her chair, her whole body tingling with anticipation. She stroked the name at the bottom of the column, imagining it was his naked chest she was touching. She glanced at the clock on her desk. Not long now. Her phone rang and the smile slipped from her face. Ian.

'Hello love, how's it going?'

'It's hard with so few staff in, but we're getting there. What have you been up to?' She forced herself to sound interested.

'Oh you know us furloughed-types, we just sit around watching TV and laughing at the rest of you still going to work.' Angie could hear the laughter in his voice and couldn't help a slight smile emerging despite her irritation.

'What have you really been doing?'

'Prepped all the veg for dinner and cleared out the shed this morning. You got a good team today?'

'The best.'

She paused a moment and loyalty won out over truth.

'Ian... I'm sorry I had to furlough you, you know that, don't you?'

'Course I do love. Don't be daft. I'll get my turn at work in a few weeks.'

She glanced at the clock again. Almost lunchtime. 'I've got to go. We've got a shipment due in any minute. I'll see you this evening.'

Putting the phone down, she checked her face quickly in the mirror and strode out of the office onto the warehouse floor. She'd timed it perfectly. The workers below were all filing out of the door heading to the canteen for lunch. All except one. Jack was leaning against one of the shelves watching her as she descended the stairs.

'Not hungry?' she asked, nodding towards the door as it banged shut behind the last worker to leave.

'Plenty hungry,' he said, 'But they don't serve what I want in the canteen.'

It was a terrible line, but she smiled anyway, knowing exactly why he was there.

'Did you find somewhere?'

Angie smiled and crooked her finger. He followed her through the warehouse to the deserted loading bay and pulled her into his arms as soon as they were concealed by the half-loaded lorry. One kiss later, he had her pressed against the wall, skirt hitched up, his fingers fumbling with his zip. Then he froze.

'What about the cameras?'

She tugged his zip down impatiently.

'Out of action,' she muttered against his mouth. 'System's down.'

'You're a genius,' he panted, finally freeing himself from his trousers. 'Only you could furlough your husband and keep your lover at work.'

Angie didn't reply. She didn't want to think about Ian. Not now.

On the other side of the building, the security guard waved goodbye to the engineer as he got back in his van.

On the wall in the loading bay a red light blinked and a faint whirring sound could just be heard over the noises floating up from below.

First published in *Makarelle, 2021*

I Am Not Who I Am

Trudie gazed out of the window of the bus as it pulled up outside Shoreditch Town Hall. *Charlotte can't pronounce Marylebone #loveyourimperfections* an advert proclaimed. She sympathised with Charlotte, Marylebone was hard to say. Her advert would have read *Trudie is a frustrated spinster*, but she didn't see that as an imperfection because the two descriptions weren't linked. Who wanted to share their poky flat with someone who didn't understand the purpose of a laundry basket and who left a trail of dirty clothes for her to follow in a miserable parody of her favourite musical? Unlike Dorothy, there was no Emerald City with its wish-granting wizard at the end of Trudie's yellow brick road, just a soggy pile of green towels on the bathroom floor. No, she thought, her frustration arose from their assumption that it was acceptable to use her then move on without even being polite enough to inform her of the fact. That frustration was the reason she'd reinvented herself. Mousy Trudie Brown had disappeared, to be replaced by red-headed 'Madame Jasmine' whose trailing scarves floated around her like confused butterflies. Trudie was still there if one looked closely enough, but Jasmine concealed her fairly well.

Her tarot cards were tucked safely into her bag and the flea market silver locket hung over the patchwork gypsy dress created from the clothes Alistair 'left behind' when she threw him out. That particular ending – the first in a long line – came after she found texts from his perfectly manicured secretary. Elaine – she of the muted make-up, perfectly styled hair and cut-glass vowels – set Trudie's teeth grinding from the moment they met. *Don't worry dahling, not everyone is cut out for university.* Alistair came home to find the locks changed and a single box of his possessions tipped on its side on the communal lawn.

'You need to be more discerning,' her mother told her.

Trudie agreed, despite not knowing what 'discerning' meant.

Things will be different this time. Soon, I'll have enough money for a new life and it's all thanks to Hugo.

The man sitting opposite smiled at her and she returned it with interest.

Yes. This time things will definitely be different.

* * *

She'd had her tarot cards spread out on the table of a greasy spoon in Stepney when Hugo had arrived for their meeting.

'Lovers, Ace of Cups, Hermit,' he said, dropping languidly into the chair opposite her. 'You're going to fall madly in love with a *very* handsome man.' He grinned crookedly, clearly attempting to look charming. 'Ace of Cups – there's a new relationship on the way. Not necessarily romantic, but certainly to your benefit. And lastly, The Hermit – wise enough to know when to let go of your old life and open yourself up to travelling along a new path. I'd say your life was about to change for the better.'

His smile broadened. Trudie allowed herself to return it.

'I ain't finished,' she said, emphasising the unfamiliar accent. 'You only get the full picture wiv all six.'

He used the Lovers to flip over the remaining cards.

'Five of Cups, Wheel of Fortune, Seven of Swords. Go on then, what else does that tell you about me?'

'You don't learn from your mistakes and you'll always take a chance to get what you want. Somethin's botherin' you. Or it could be a warnin' of danger - s'hard to tell sometimes. Anyways, this one's meant to be a readin' for me not you.'

'I'm not so sure,' he said, extending his hand. 'Hugo Mortenson at your service. You might have been looking for your own future, but those cards pretty much sum up my present situation. Thank-you for agreeing to meet. It was a complete godsend when I saw your advert. Let me buy you a coffee and tell you all about it. It might be advantageous for you – if not, we can forget all about it as long as you agree to let me take you to dinner to compensate for wasting your time. I never could resist a redhead.'

Trudie smiled to herself. The hair dye had been a good idea.

'I'm Jasmine. Or Madame Jasmine, if I'm workin'.' She winked at him.

'My grandmother is into all this spiritual business and I need someone to persuade her to give me some money. It's my trust fund, but she thinks she can control me, just because she controls the money. I want her to release enough for me to be independent and if the cards tell her to give me the money, I believe she will. There'd be a commission for you, obviously. If it works. What do you think? Would you be game?'

Trudie delayed her response, trying to use the spirits to

'see' him, but he was still hard to read. She felt odd inside and didn't like that she couldn't explain why.

'Ask the cards,' he said, seeing her hesitation. 'Let me draw for you and then you can decide.'

Silently, Trudie shuffled the deck and spread them out. Hugo pulled out three cards and placed them upright in front of her. The Lovers, The Wheel of Fortune and the Seven of Swords.

'Well we seem to be well-matched in one area!' He traced the vein on the back of her hand.

Slowly, Trudie nodded. The cards had warned him. It wasn't her fault if he ignored them.

'OK. You're on.'

He lifted her hand and kissed it with a self-satisfied smirk.

'I'll be in touch.'

* * *

The evening before she was due to see Hugo's grandmother, Trudie read the cards again, trying to confirm she was doing the right thing, but sensing something was going wrong.

'Hugo, it's that Seven of Swords again. I'm positive it's a warnin'. I'm not sure I wanna do this. We could be meddlin' with somethin' dangerous.'

'I'm coming over.'

He listened to her halting speech in silence, then turned away. Of course she was free to change her mind and he absolutely understood her fears, but he desperately needed the money from his grandmother. Only she could help him. His words caught in his throat, then he pulled her into his arms and kissed her with all the tenderness she had once desired. In the exhausted aftermath, as they lay together in a tangled web of sheets, his arm a dead weight across her body, she whispered that she would keep her word and help him if that was truly what he wanted.

Something stirred in the shadow of the bed. Disturbed by the movement, Trudie moaned in a sleep that was suddenly filled with indistinguishable faces leering at her. A slight breeze tickled her splayed leg and she shivered and withdrew it into the shelter of the bedcovers. As silence fell once more upon the darkened room, something stirred again, more quietly this time, keen not to draw attention to itself. It watched the sleeping figures and it waited.

Hugo left, having reminded her which bus she had to catch and given strict instructions about what to say when she arrived. He had keenly (and painfully) impressed it upon her that she must make what she said sound natural. She rubbed her arm, where the reddened skin still flickered like the dying flames of the coal fires she'd grown up with. He'd not meant to hurt her, he assured her, he was just so passionate about this undertaking and she hadn't quite struck the right note of casual revelation when they practised it. He was frustrated and simply gripped her arm too tight. He didn't even know he was twisting it until she let out a squeak of protest. He immediately let go and apologised, kissing it better and soothing away the hurt, but reminded her, between kisses, that she *had* to convince his grandmother to release some of the capital. She didn't need reminding. She knew what had to be done.

* * *

Trudie looked around the grand room she had been shown into. Dimly lit by a central chandelier, the shadows in the corners menaced and hemmed her in. She was a tiny fly in a web that was closing in around her, trapping her until she didn't know which way to turn. Every twist and struggle only tightened the invisible threads keeping her pinned there. She was more convinced than ever that coming here had been a mistake. She thought again about the warning from the cards: had it really been for Hugo?

'So you're the tarot reader my grandson has been raving about, are you?

Mrs Arnold was a tall woman, whose body defied what Trudie knew to be her age. The woman had outlasted nineteen Prime Ministers and had outlived most of them as well. She wouldn't look out of place in a discus circle and yet for all her physical strength, she had an unwavering belief in the non-physical world of the occult and it was this Hugo was expecting Jasmine to use to his advantage.

'Yes Grandmama. This is Madame Jasmine. She's very highly recommended.'

'Thank-you Hugo. I'm neither so old, nor so senile that I can't make up my own mind!'

Her grandson seemed to shrink beneath her words.

'I'm sorry Grandmama, I didn't mean to imply —'

'Oh for heaven's sake, just leave us!'

There was a brief pause after the door clicked, then Mrs Arnold turned to her guest.

'Hello again, Trudie dear. Are you ready?'

Trudie swallowed hard.

'Are you sure you want to do this?'

'Absolutely my dear. We've had this conversation already and I have no doubts. My grandson is not a nice young man and has to be stopped. He must pay for his sins, for they have found him out. As he has not broken any laws – save those of morality and decency – we must make recourse to other methods of justice. There's a plethora of broken hearts already: yours was not the only abortion I've organised and goodness only knows how many fatherless children there are out there. I had hoped he'd settle down with a nice girl, but he's always had rather a taste for the common woman. If he'd even recognised you that day in the café, I might have reconsidered, but he has no idea who you are, even now. No my dear, I'm afraid my mind is quite made up. As I told you last year and again last week, you must simply trust my judgement. Hugo is reckless and irresponsible and he needs to be stopped before someone else gets hurt.'

Mrs Arnold took a seat opposite Trudie and selected her cards.

'Shall we begin?'

Trudie laid the cards out between them and watched as Mrs Arnold made her selection. Turning them over, a gasp escaped from between her tightly pressed lips. The Seven of Swords. She pushed the cards away.

'I can't do this.'

'Don't be ridiculous, child! We agreed he had to be stopped.'

'I know, but —'

'Don't dither, girl! He has to pay for what he did to you and the others.'

'I know.' Trudie's hands fluttered over the cards. "it's just...that card keeps coming up. I thought it was warning *him* of danger, but now I'm not sure... maybe it's *us* who need to listen to the cards.'

'You're being ridiculous.' Mrs Arnold's voice rose in parallel with her anger. 'Is this about money? Because if it is, I warn you not to test me. I offered you a fair price which you agreed to. If you back out now, you'll get nothing. Do you hear me? Nothing!'

Her voice ricocheted around the high ceiling, rebounding off the bookcases, then dissolved into the shadows that seemed to have no source. The silence that descended over the room sucked everything into it. Mrs Arnold looked stunned by her uncharacteristic loss of control.

'Go.'

The strangled whisper shifter Trudie's attention back to the cards. With dismay, she realised they were still spread across the table, drawing the negative energy into themselves. When she gathered them up, they seemed to vibrate in her hands and she launched them into the bag, heedless of how they fell. Panic flooded through her. She needed to escape.

* * *

Back on the bus, Trudie clutched the bag to her chest. There was no money to start her new life, but perhaps she could move anyway. She could rent a small flat somewhere. Anywhere quiet and a long way from London. Despite the warmth of the summer evening, she shivered. She'd felt uneasy since she left the Arnold house and couldn't shake the feeling she was being followed.

'It's nothing,' she told herself sternly, tightening her grip on the bag. 'You're just being paranoid.'

Shifting the bag to her arm, she reached out and rang the bell. Nodding her thanks to the driver, she stepped off the bus and headed for home.

She didn't see the darkness that slithered behind her. Not when it hid in the shadows of the evening. Not when it slipped silently through the door of her flat.

The Date

25th June 2019

I am floating, weightless. Drifting on a sea of never-ending peace. I am alone and it feels wonderful to be free. And yet. Something is keeping me tethered in place. A piece of string? No, not string. It's thicker than string. What's it called? A tube. That's it, a tube. I don't want to be tethered and I pull at it. I'm almost free of it when hands grab hold of me and wrest it from my grip. Stop it! You don't understand! I have to go. But they are too strong for me. Pain lances through my chest and I cannot stifle the involuntary gasp that escapes me. There's a sharp scrape on the back of my hand and a sense of calm floods through me. My body relaxes against my wishes, bringing with it a return to the darkness. I can't fight it. In many ways I don't want to. I will go where it takes me.

19th December 2018

. . .

I've never had much luck with men, so when I first see Jamie across the crowded nightclub floor, I don't give him a second glance. He's way out of my league and I'm not really in the game of voluntary humiliation. I'm no more than a solid 7 and he's a definite 10. Dexter nudges me.

'I saw you looking!'

'Shut up.'

'He's looking at you, you know.'

I can't help myself. I glance up. He's right. The next moment, Jamie is by my side offering me a drink. He stays with us the rest of the night, buys me drinks, compliments my outfit. (I can't remember anyone except Dex ever doing that before and Dex doesn't count. He's my best mate. He has to be nice to me)

'I don't like him,' Dex says as we share a cab home. 'He's too full of himself. Smarmy git.'

'You're just jealous,' I tell him.

23rd December 2018

It's our first date. Jamie's been texting me non-stop since we met and he's brought me to his favourite restaurant for dinner. I've never been on a date where the man has been so solicitous. Before I've even had chance to look at the menu, he's ordered my meal and a bottle of wine.

'I hope you don't mind, 't's just that the seafood pasta in here is to die for. I'd hate for you to miss out on it.'

'Of course not, don't be silly.'

I don't want to tell him that I don't really like seafood and I'd have preferred a G&T. I'm sure it will be fine and it is. The sauce is lovely and I manage to eat a few of the prawns.

'No dessert thanks, Jess couldn't even finish the pasta! It's so filling, isn't it?'

2nd March 2019

'I don't understand what your problem is.'

'Would you like it if I had a female friend that I constantly went for a drink with, alone?'

'Well...I suppose not, but it's Dex! We've been friends since we were kids.'

'And how many girlfriends has he had in that time?'

'I don't know. A few?'

'He's in love with you, you know. I don't trust him not to make a move on you.'

'You're being ridiculous!'

'Is it ridiculous to not want another man pawing over your girlfriend?'

'No...but Dex wouldn't do that. He's not like that!'

'I'm just saying, maybe you shouldn't go out with him so often. When it's just the two of you I mean. You might give him the wrong idea and if he made a move it would ruin your friendship, wouldn't it? You don't want that, do you?'

'I suppose not.'

'And I'd do the same for you, you know. If there was someone you didn't want me to see. I think it's best for everyone if you put a little bit of distance between you. I know he doesn't like me.'

'Don't be___'

'Don't lie for him, Jess. He knows how much we love each other and I'm a threat to him. It's OK, I understand.'

. . .

23rd April 2019

'I'm sorry Jess. I shouldn't have done it, but you drove me to it. There's only so much a man can take, you know.'

'We were only talking. He knows I have a boyfriend.'

'I'm sure you did sweetheart, but you were giving him mixed signals weren't you.'

'Was I? How?'

'If you tell a man you have a boyfriend, but then keep talking to him, you're hinting that you might still be interested in him.'

'How does talking about cars mean I'm interested in sleeping with him?'

'What?'

'That's what we were talking about. He was telling me about his new car. We're colleagues, Jamie, we talk to each other. I couldn't just walk off, that would have been rude.'

'But it's OK to be rude to me? Your boyfriend? Just leaving me at the table on my own while you chat up another man?'

'You weren't on your own. You could have talked to everyone else. I only went to get a round of drinks.'

'You carried on talking to him after though, didn't you? You were flirting with everyone tonight. Even Dex, who you say you're supposedly not interested in.'

'I'm not interested in Dex, or anyone else. And even if I were, it doesn't excuse what you did.'

'You're absolutely right and I'm sorry. Please forgive me darling, I promise it won't ever happen again. I just went a bit crazy, you know? I love you so much. Please don't leave me.'

24th June 2019

. . .

'Where the hell have you been?'

'I had to work late. Didn't you get my text?'

'Oh I got your text alright, I just don't believe it. You're seeing someone else aren't you? That's why you're late. Don't lie to me, Jess!'

I don't know what to say to pacify him anymore. Whatever I say will only make things worse, but I have to try.

'I'm not lying. I had to finish typing up a report that had to be sent today. You can see the email if you want.'

'Oh I don't doubt you'll have covered your tracks. You're a conniving little bitch aren't you?'

My face is flecked with his spit as the words pour forth from him, a never-ending stream of vile words. By now I know where this is heading and I know that my only course of action is to stay quiet. The more I try to defend myself the worse it becomes. This isn't how I saw my future all those months ago. I still don't know what I did wrong, but I must have done something. None of his previous girlfriends have provoked him to such rage, so it must be me. I wish he'd just tell me what it was. When the darkness comes, I welcome it.

26th June 2019

I am floating on that peaceful sea again, but this time, whilst I am still alone, I feel anchored. Safe. The tube is still there, but it's not that holding me down now. There's something else doing that. Something warm and comforting. A hand. A large hand, holding mine. It feels so right and I want to know who it belongs to.

'Doctor! She's coming round.'

I force my eyelids to open. They don't want to co-operate, but I am determined. I blink at the harsh light overhead.

'Hello you. Nice of you to join us.'

Dex. I smile.

First published on my website, 2020

Spes Mea In Deo*

Daisy sat plucking at the frayed edges of her cardigan sleeve, red-rimmed eyes staring, but unseeing. She had come here to find peace, but she was beginning to think that maybe there was none to be found. If she couldn't find it in a deserted graveyard in a quiet village in rural Essex, then where would she? She certainly wasn't finding it in her new house, which was why she'd fled from the loneliness that morning and driven aimlessly around until she'd stumbled across the church. Her siblings thought she was mad and maybe she was, but she needed to do something to shake herself free of the slump into which she'd fallen since Luke's passing. Nothing else had worked, so maybe moving away, out of the house they'd shared and beginning again somewhere new, would be the answer she was looking for.

It's not fair, she thought angrily. *At my age I should have been planning children and discussing childcare options, not thinking about funeral plans.*

She wasn't sure which piece of unfairness was the worst, that Luke had died, or that he'd done so before they'd had the opportunity to have children. *At least if we'd had kids I'd have a part of him with me still.* She groaned and rested her head in her hands.

'Oh Luke,' she whispered. 'What am I going to do?'

The sound of someone clearing their throat startled her and she looked up to see a kindly face above her, its owner wearing a concerned expression.

'Forgive me for intruding,' the voice was gentle, 'But you appear to be in some distress. Is there anything I can do for you?'

'Not unless you have the power to bring back the dead,' Daisy said, with a tired smile.

'Oh, my dear,' the woman said. 'May I?' She gestured to the empty space beside Daisy. When Daisy nodded, she settled onto the bench. 'Would you like to talk about it?'

There was something about her that invited confidences and Daisy found herself pouring out her story.

'Luke and I met at work – his desk was opposite mine and I kept coming back from lunch to find a bar of my favourite chocolate by my computer, or sometimes a little posy of flowers if I was having a bad day. He always denied all knowledge but I kind of guessed it was him. Then one day there were tickets to a play I'd mentioned wanting to see and a little note with them saying I could take anyone I wanted with the extra ticket, but he'd be happy to keep me company if I wanted him to. Of course, I said yes and then a year later he took me to the same theatre and proposed. A year after that, we got married.

Three years ago we started trying for a baby. When it didn't happen straight away we tried to be patient, but then we had some tests done and they picked up that there was an issue with Luke. When they did further tests, they discovered he had cancer. It was too advanced and too aggressive for them to do anything and he died six months ago. He was only thirty-three. I couldn't bear to carry on living in our house so I sold it and bought one here instead and now I don't know if I did the right thing.'

'You poor girl,' the woman said. 'You have had a rough time of it, haven't you? Is he buried here?'

Daisy shook her head.

'We scattered his ashes in the sea nearby though. We used to come and sail at Brightlingsea and it's where we were happiest, so it seemed appropriate. That's where my new house is, so I go to the beach and talk to him sometimes. The locals must think I'm mad! Do you have relatives here?' she asked.

An odd expression crossed the woman's face as she nodded.

'My husband, my daughter and all three of my sons are buried or remembered here,' she said.

'I'm so sorry,' Daisy said. 'I didn't mean to prattle on about my loss.'

'It was a long time ago,' the woman reassured her, patting her hand. 'My husband used to be the rector of this parish.'

Daisy looked around her. Across the graveyard the church rose up, a solid edifice of stone pilfered from a long abandoned Roman villa that had once stood nearby. Even though she had no particular faith, its presence reassured and comforted her. The red tiled roof and the little tower at one end blocked the attached cemetery from the road behind, giving the place an air of isolation, as though the building stood sentinel, keeping the outside world from intruding on the peace beyond it.

'What happened to your sons... if you don't mind me asking?' she added quickly.

The woman waved away her concern.

'Not at all. It's been a few years now. They were all in the army you see. Killed in action. Losing them like that broke my husband's heart. He followed them three years after the first two were killed. They said it was the flu that took him, but I know it was a broken heart. Those boys were everything to us and for two of them to be taken within four months of each other was downright cruel. First our youngest and then Giles, our middle boy. I raged against God for taking them, but my Charlie kept his faith. "Peggy," he said, "we have to trust in God and be grateful we still have our Francis and our Meggie and that He has not taken them as well." He didn't know that God would soon take our eldest too; he died before that happened and I'm glad for it. That would have been a cross even he might have failed to bear. Our Meggie had a good life in the end though - saw the old age denied her brothers. God made us wait until we were well into middle age before he gave us children and then he only let us keep our boys for a short time. I wasn't sure I wanted to believe in a God who did that, but Charlie persevered with me and I'm glad he did for I made my peace with Him in the end. My only worry is who will remember my boys when I'm gone. There'll be no-one to bring them flowers.'

'How long did it take to find that peace?' Daisy asked. 'It's been six months since Luke died and I'm still angry with the world for taking him and I'm angrier still with him for leaving me behind. I thought if I moved away I might find that peace you're talking about, but it's not happened yet.'

'Give it time,' the woman said. 'It will come to you eventually and the pain will weaken its grip on you. I promise it will get easier to bear.'

It was nothing Daisy hadn't heard before, but for some reason she believed it coming from this woman who had borne such loss and still found a way to survive.

'Thank-you,' she said, rising from the seat and stretching. 'I'll leave you in peace now, but you have no idea how much you've helped today.'

The woman gave her a gentle smile.

'Any time, my dear,' she said. 'I'm always here.'

As she got back in the car, Daisy decided to treat herself to lunch in the pub that stood at the top of the road leading to the little church.

As she waited for her food to arrive, she got chatting to some of the locals about the village and why she was there.

'I'm glad I came though,' she said. 'Luke and I drove through here a few times, but we never stopped. It's a shame – he'd have loved your little church. He was fascinated by old buildings.'

For a moment the men looked confused.

'Our church is a modern building,' one of them said.

'You must mean the old church,' another broke in. 'Bottom of the hill by the war memorial.'

'That's the one,' Daisy agreed. 'Red roof and a pretty little cemetery at the back.'

'That church has no roof. Hasn't had for nearly forty years. It burnt down in 1971. Nothing but a ruin now.'

'But I spoke to the old rector's wife,' Daisy explained. 'She told me about losing her sons in the war and then her husband a few years later. She was too old for it to have been Afghanistan, so I assume it must have been the first Gulf War, so what would that be? Early 90s?'

'Someone's been having you on, love,' the man behind the bar said, frowning. 'I've lived in this place all my life and we've had no vicar who lost children in a war in all that time.'

Daisy frowned.

'How strange. She seemed like such a nice lady as well.'

'Well, like anywhere, we have our fair share of oddballs in the village. I dare say she meant no harm. I wouldn't worry too much if I were you.'

But it continued to play on Daisy's mind as she ate her steak. The woman had seemed too kind to have been lying to her and even if they were right about her, it didn't explain their comment about the church being ruined. They'd been straight-faced enough but Daisy knew what some small villages were like about winding up visitors and the church had definitely been there this morning. When she got back in the car however, something made her turn her back on the road to Brightlingsea and retrace her route to the little church.

Stepping onto the stony path that led to the entry door, Daisy stopped abruptly. The wooden door she'd noticed this morning had gone, as had the roof and the neat path she had walked on. Jagged edges of stone reached up to the blue sky and the path was overgrown with tangled plants that tugged at her ankles. Her heart thudding, Daisy passed through the exposed interior of the ruined building and out to the little cemetery. The graves, which this morning had looked mostly pristine and new, were now a mix of modern and old headstones, most of which were covered with moss and lichen, their occupants having lain unvisited for many years. The bench where Daisy had sat and chatted with the old lady was still there, but the triple-headed grave in front of it now looked a shadow of what it had been this morning, the white stone faded, grubbied and cracked.

Daisy crossed over to it and stooped to look at the inscriptions. Giles and Rowland Prichard had both died in 1915. Next to them was the smaller headstone of their sister Margaret who had lived to see the second half of the century and on her other side lay Charles Collwyn Prichard and his wife Margaret, their dates of death 1918 and 1921 respectively.

Daisy rocked back on her heels and stared at the words. She straightened and rested her hand on the flat edge at the top of the headstone and whispered a promise.

'I'll bring flowers next time I come.

. . .

*My hope is in God

First published in *A Cinque Port Collection*, 2022

Eagle One Eagle Two

I need to write this down. If I don't, I'll forget it happened. Forget it was ever more than a story. I'm a writer by trade, but the truth is far stranger than any fiction I could ever invent. Isn't it always though?

I walked past the hotel and shuddered. They were doing it again. Looking at me. I mean, obviously they weren't. How could they? They were made of stone. Stone can't look at you. So why did it feel like that's exactly what they were doing? I gave myself a metaphorical shake. They were just decorations. Nothing more than stone statues designed to make the hotel entrance look grander. And as for the one on the roof, well that was pure eighteenth-century patriotism at its very best. The hotel was originally a mansion, built by the wealthy mayor of the town in the days of George III and the architecture was typical of the grandiose posturing such people preferred, with eagles guarding the gates, Britannia on the roof and an abundance of columns and white stucco adorning the smart red brickwork. Everything about it screamed wealthy, imperial Britain. It was a truly beautiful building, but those statues gave me the creeps. I'd only lived in Launceston a few weeks and already I didn't like walking past them at night. Deep down, I knew it was only my over-active imagination having 'fun' with my nerves, but still.

As I reached the opening in the wall which gave access to the outdoor dining area, a woman dressed in black and with a veil covering her face, passed me on the other side of it. A faint waft of lavender drifted behind her and the scent made me turn, as I always do, to inhale it again. It's such a soothing smell: it reminds me of my grandmother.

The woman had disappeared. She'd had no time to enter the bar or the hotel. She was just... gone.

Not giving myself time to think, I turned on my heel and almost sprinted through the old gatehouse and onto the green of the castle grounds beyond. *I was mistaken. There was no woman. Or if there was, she was simply hidden behind something.* The sun was beating down and I'd been busy all morning building furniture. I was just hungry. That had to be it. Just my tired, hungry brain misinterpreting the signals it had been sent.

I bought myself a pasty from the shop on the High Street and sat by the war memorial to eat it. I know, I know... I sat in the sun in Cornwall eating a Cornish pasty, but honestly, I don't care. The ones from Malcolm Barnecutt's are so nice it's worth being a walking (or in this case, sitting) cliché. I closed my eyes, allowing the glorious weather to chase away the last of the fear that insisted on lurking in the furthest recess of my mind. I scolded myself. How could I have let my imagination run away with me so badly? I'd been in the hotel for several drinks and a meal. I'd spoken to the owners, who were lovely by the way, and on not one of these occasions had there been any hint of ghostly old women. In the short time I'd been in Launceston, I'd realised that one thing the locals were always happy to tell you about was any hint of a ghost. Even if they claim to be completely sceptical themselves, the Cornish know their local history and the accompanying ghosts and I'm pretty sure that one of their favourites past-times is scaring the emmets. Technically, I no longer count as an emmet as I live here and am doing my best to learn the language, but I'm also clearly not Cornish born and bred, so I'm probably still fair game when it comes to the spooky stories. My next door neighbour certainly takes great delight in sharing them with me.

Wiping the last flakes of pastry from the corners of my mouth, I stretched and rose from my seat. For a moment I debated whether to take the longer route back to my flat, past the church and down the narrow path that ran alongside it. It was steeper but it would mean I didn't have to walk past the hotel again. Deciding I was being ridiculous, I jammed my sunglasses firmly back up my nose and headed towards the castle.

'Dydh da.'

Two voices made me jump as the contrast between the shadowy coolness of the gatehouse and the brilliant sunlight momentarily disorientated me. I squinted at the two small figures before my brain processed what they'd said.

'Dydh da.' I smiled apologetically. 'That's about the extent of my Cornish, I'm afraid.'

The two fair haired boys grinned at me.

'Emmet?'

'No, I live here. It's the first time I've heard anyone speaking Cornish though. I'm guessing you must be local. Are you fluent?'

The boys nodded and broke into a stream of Cornish, taking it in turns to gabble away at me.'

I laughed and held up my hands. 'Very impressive boys, but I didn't understand a word!'

They looked at each other and smiled.

'You saw her, didn't you?'

I frowned. 'Who?'

'The old lady.'

I felt my feet root themselves to the ground even as I felt the urge to flee.

'We were sitting up there and we saw you react.'

'Did she say anything?'

'Did she look old?'

I held up my hands. 'I thought I'd imagined her.'

'No, she's real. Well, as real as a ghost can be. She's the old owner's mother. He killed himself, you know. She haunts the house looking for him.'

That caught my attention. It certainly hadn't been in the potted history of the hotel I'd been given.

'That's terrible.'

The boys looked at each other again.

'They say it's because he had his heart broken.'

'He fell in love with a woman and they got engaged. Then she just disappeared. Left him all alone and he drowned himself in the Kensey down by the packhorse bridge.'

I had a feeling I was being wound up. At that point the river is barely more than a stream. The boys seemed to sense my scepticism and hastened to assure me of the truth of their tale.

'Apparently, he just lay down with his face in the water one night. They found him the next day.'

Poor lady, I thought. I said goodbye to the boys and continued down the hill, resisting the urge to check if the eagles were still watching me. Just before I turned the corner I glanced back. The boys were gone, but the eagles were there, heads turned away from each other, watching the hill in both directions. I walked quickly round the bend and back down the road to my flat.

A few days later, I decided to go for a drink. It was a beautiful summer's evening and the view from the hotel terrace was glorious at sunset. I'd been cooped up inside all day and felt I deserved a treat. I walked slowly up the hill, anticipating the cold notes of blueberries and raspberries in the Eagle One gin I'd promised myself if I stayed at my desk all day.

As I sat watching the sun sink slowly behind the trees, I noticed a dark figure alone at a table in the corner of the terrace. For a moment, I looked at my glass: it was still almost full. I looked over again. She was still there. As I processed this, she caught my eye and nodded an acknowledgment. Tentatively I smiled and she beckoned me over. I picked up my drink and took the few steps across the terrace.

'Do I present such a fearsome picture?' she asked.

Her face was deeply lined with age, but now I'd established she was flesh and blood, it held no horrors for me and I shook my head, half-laughing at myself.

'Not in the least. It's only that I caught sight of you a few days ago and you seemed to just vanish and then I was told you were a ghost. A joke, I realise, but it was a bit of a shock to see you sitting there.'

Her answering laugh was dry and brittle, like the rustle of old paper.

'I'm old but I'm not dead yet.'

'My imagination runs away with me sometimes. I'm a writer you see, so it's mostly an advantage, but it does mean I'm easy to frighten. I don't particularly like statues at the best of times and this place is old and it's Cornwall and there's ghosts everywhere. You get the idea! My neighbour thinks it's great fun to torment me with ghost stories.'

'And was it your neighbour who told you I was a ghost?'

I shook my head. 'No. That particular gem came courtesy of two little boys. I bumped into them just outside the gates and they took great delight in telling me the story of the old lady whose son had killed himself, because the woman he loved left him. They said you were his mother still haunting the hotel and looking for him.'

My smile faded away as I took in the expression on her face. Her hand clamped over mine, her grip surprisingly strong given her frail appearance.

'That's no story. My son did kill himself many years ago for that reason, but there's none left alive now who would remember. What did the boys look like?'

'Very like each other. Blonde curly hair. Twins maybe?'

The hand gripping mine convulsed and she made a choking sound.

'One of them had a scar on his cheek.'

Now she mentioned it, I remembered the mark clearly and I nodded.

'That's right.'

'You can't possibly have spoken to them. Those boys are dead.'

I stared at her, feeling the perspiration slide down my back.

'Dead?' I echoed.

'Murdered by a madwoman over a hundred years ago.' I took an unsteady sip from my glass as she continued. 'Local witch. Didn't like the fact her beloved son had taken up with a woman who already had two children. He didn't care, loved them like they were his own, but the witch knew what the woman was really like. On the surface she was loving and kind, but the witch knew. She knew the woman was only pretending. Her son was wealthy. Owned a beautiful house. The woman had nothing. The son wasn't a good-looking boy and he was quiet and shy. Some said it was because his mother had too firm a hand over him. She'd cast a spell on him to keep him close to her. The spell wasn't strong enough though and he fell for the woman. His mother was mad with jealousy. The woman was going to take her son away from her. She was going to hurt him. The witch gave her fair warning. She told the woman she knew what she was about. The woman protested of course: said she truly loved the witch's son. But the witch knew better. She had to protect her son. She cursed the woman and her sons, but the curse went wrong. When her son saw the new statues on the house he knew what his mother had done and he swore he would never forgive her. She told him he was overreacting, that she'd done it to protect him. The woman had never really loved him, but he wouldn't listen. The witch was worried, so she renewed the spell that kept them bound together, but her son escaped and they found him the next morning, face down in the river.'

I swear I didn't make a sound, but she must have felt my hand twitch, for she tightened her grip on it.

'The spell worked though. The statues remain so the son remains, still wanting to be close to his love. And because the son remains, so must the mother. I've been here a long time, my dear and will be here a while longer.'

She released my hand abruptly and left me alone at the table. The hotel's owner suddenly appeared at my elbow.

'Are you alright?' he asked. 'Mrs Kendall can be a little intense sometimes, but she's generally harmless. Has she been telling you ghost stories about this place?'

I nodded. 'Who is she?'

He frowned. 'She came with the hotel when we bought it. She's a permanent resident and has a suite on the top floor. We only ever really see her for meals.'

I handed him my now empty gin glass, feeling the need to return home to the safety of my flat. Had she been telling me the truth or was she, like my neighbour, entertaining herself at my expense?

As I walked past the hotel entrance I glanced up at Britannia, then my eye fell on the eagles. I stared at the nearest one. It gazed back, unblinking.

This story was inspired by the Charles Causley poems, *Eagle One, Eagle Two* and *Miller's End*.

First published in *Makarelle*, 2021

The Grave Man

The man strode through the graveyard, his gaze swinging from side to side, taking in the lichen covered stones basking in the shade of the yew trees that burst through the hardened earth. Frost shimmered on the dark leaves and he pulled his scarf tighter around his throat. He'd forgotten how cold winters in England could be and not for the first time that day he asked himself if he'd done the right thing in coming home. Funny how he still thought of it as home, despite not having set foot in the country for years.

In one corner of the churchyard, a small group of people were gathered like crows around a carcass. Idle curiosity propelled him in their direction and he hovered at the rear of the assembly, listening to the solemn intonations of the vicar.

'In the midst of life we are in death…'

Very true. He'd been alive for sixty-five years and had felt dead for approximately thirty-five of them.

'Did you know him? My grandfather, I mean.'

The speaker was a boy of about fifteen. The man shook his head. The boy's face fell and he felt compelled to continue the conversation.

'Were you close?'

'No, I never actually met him. He abandoned my Gran and my Mum when Mum was only little. Gran said he walked out on them and then said he didn't want anything to do with her or Mum anymore. I can't understand why someone would do that. What kind of man doesn't want to know his own kid?'

'If you feel so strongly about it, why are you here?'

The boy shrugged. 'It's still family, you know? I just thought if you'd known him, you might know why he left.'

'Sorry kid, can't help, I'm afraid. Don't judge him too harshly though, there might be circumstances your Mum didn't know. He may not have had a choice.'

'There's always a choice.'

The boy was right. A lifetime of regrets had taught the man there was always a choice, even if it didn't feel like it at the time. He'd had thirty years to think about how he might have acted differently. He couldn't have stayed, they were too different for that and if he hadn't left when he did, he'd never have met Barbara. Barbara. A single tear rolled down his cheek, following the twin contours of old age and grief. She'd made him happy over the years, but now he was angry with her. Angry she'd left him and angry she'd extracted such a promise from him. It was because of her he was here instead of soaking up the Spanish sun and hiding from the mistakes he'd made.

'Promise me you'll go,' she said, gripping his hand with a strength that defied her ravaged appearance.

He agreed of course. There was nothing else he could do. Couldn't deny her dying wish, could he? Not even if it meant seeing Evelyn again – he didn't have any bitterness towards her anymore, or not much anyway. They married too young, he knew that now, but it was hard to shake the feeling that she'd deliberately turned their daughter against him.

He couldn't pinpoint exactly when their marriage had

begun to fall apart; the arguments had almost crept up on them, gradually increasing in number until life became one long argument.

'I'm leaving,' she announced over breakfast. 'I'm taking Laura to my mum's.'

He begged her not to leave, but she went anyway. By Sunday evening she was back.

'I think we should give it another go. It doesn't seem right to give up so easily.'

He agreed because it was easier than arguing and because he loved his daughter. She left him for another weekend and then for a whole week, but each time she came back and insisted she wanted to try again. He no longer knew if he loved her and wasn't sure he cared either way. It wasn't until she started coming home late after work every night that he realised he'd had enough. Everything was always on her terms: it had been throughout their marriage, but he'd never minded before. Or, he considered, at least not consciously. Now, he acknowledged, there had been some simmering resentment that they spent every holiday with her family and only occasional weekends with his. On the last occasion of her leaving and returning, he'd finally made a decision.

'I can't keep on like this,' he said, 'never knowing where I am or what's happening with us is killing me. I think it's time to accept that this isn't working. I'm going to start looking for my own place.'

She begged and pleaded with him not to leave. She'd try harder to make things work. She'd stop walking out on him. She'd do anything he asked if he just stayed. He wanted to relent, to say he wouldn't leave, but he knew it was the only way he'd ever find peace. Their marriage was never going to work. They both knew that she simply wanted it to end on her terms not his, but he wanted to deny her that small victory.

A few weeks later he packed his bags and moved into his

new flat. It was further away from his daughter than he would've liked, but Evelyn had insisted that he put some distance between them.

'If we're making a break, it has to be a clean one, otherwise there's no point.'

He suspected it had more to do with not wanting him to be able to see who was at the house with her, but he didn't have the strength to argue the point, so he found himself a flat near his office, but still close enough to make seeing his daughter an easy task.

At first, things had gone smoothly and the alternate weekends he saw Laura were a joy now he didn't have to cope with Evelyn's moods alongside a wilful four year old. As the months went on however and it became clear he wasn't about confess to having made a mistake and beg to be allowed to return home, Evelyn started to make excuses about why Laura couldn't come for her allotted weekend. She had a dance show. They were going on holiday for a week. She'd been invited to a birthday party. The list went on. Eventually, the excuses ran out.

'I'm sorry, but she just doesn't want to come.' He shouldn't have been surprised, but it still stung. 'I'm not going to make her. She's old enough to make her own decisions now.'

He still sent birthday cards and presents throughout the year. None were returned, but neither were they acknowledged. Occasionally, he tried to make contact, but the answer was always the same.

'She doesn't want to see you.'

He tried again and again, but over the years he gradually accepted his daughter was lost to him. Withdrawing into himself, he eventually took a sabbatical from his job and went on a long holiday to decide what to do with the rest of his life. It was on that holiday he'd met Barbara and learnt to see the joy in things again. His sorrow about losing Laura was always there lurking in the shadows, but he learnt to live with it, moved on with his life.

Barbara wasn't able to have children, but they were both philosophical about it and threw themselves into life, going on long-haul holidays, always exploring new places and climbing their way up the career ladder with outward ease.

One day, his company had asked if he would be interested in relocating to Spain – they were opening a new office there, would he be interested in heading it up? He talked to Barbara and decided yes, he would. His new salary was enough to live on, so Barbara agreed to leave her job and go freelance. She could work anywhere as long as it had a fast internet connection and Spain sounded lovely. It would give them a whole new adventure to have together. Spanish language classes were quickly arranged and attended and within six months they'd rented out their house in England and with a generous relocation package from his company, bought a villa with a pool from where he could easily commute to his new office.

Life was going well and the problems left behind in England had in the main, remained there. He had everything he wanted until the day Barbara had broken the news she had cancer. She'd been feeling unwell for a while, but they'd dismissed it as a symptom of getting older.

He didn't take the news well, but Barbara was strong enough for them both until he felt able to cope. He kept all his fear and pain tied up inside him, watching as she struggled to keep a smile on her face, pretending he didn't see the pain she was trying to disguise.

'I'm fighting it,' she told him.' You know me, I won't go down without a fight. I think I feel a bit better today. That must be a good sign, right?'

He appreciated her trying to hide what she knew, trying to protect him from the knowledge of what was to come. It was how things had always been between them. It wasn't that he was weak, it was more that Barbara knew how much he'd been hurt in the past and consequently felt the need to protect him as much as she could. This time though, she couldn't shield him from it and as time moved slowly and painfully on, it was his turn to support her as she fluctuated between raging at the disease for slowly stripping away her dignity and fear for how he would cope when she'd gone.

'Will you go back to England? You could do, now you've retired.'

He shook his head slowly, considering and dismissing the idea in a moment.

'No. My life's been here for the past twenty years. Where would I go if I went back?'

'You could go and see Laura.'

All the feelings of despair and rejection he'd pushed down deep within himself rose to the surface wrapped in a patchwork blanket of panic and fear. Barbara smiled weakly at him, the effort visible in the creases that lined her thin face.

'It's been long enough. She might have changed her mind by now. Promise me you'll try.'

He nodded and after the funeral, reluctantly booked himself a flight to London. His hotel in his old home-town organised, there was nothing left for him to do but sit back and agonise over what awaited him. To give himself something to do, he scoured the internet to find any traces of his former family online and discovered Evelyn had died some years earlier. Their old house had been sold, but Laura's address was easy enough to trace once he'd discovered her married name.

His stroll through the graveyard had been a way of buying time for himself, to put off the point of meeting. He hadn't contacted Laura ahead of time, not wanting to give her chance to tell him not to bother coming, hoping that the shock of seeing him would prompt her to talk to him, even if it was only to tell him why she'd continually refused to see him all those years before. He'd just given himself a stern talking to and set off with renewed purpose, when the funeral caught his eye and he felt himself drawn to it.

The man felt the teenager's eyes still on him and he pulled himself out of his reminiscing and forced himself to smile.

'Like I said, son, there might be two sides to it – there usually is.'

'I'd like to think so. Mum doesn't know why he didn't want to see her and Gran wouldn't talk about him after a while. It would be nice to think there was a reason for it all.'

The man inclined his head towards the grave.

'What was he called?'

'Ronnie. Ronnie Westmacott.'

The man stared at him, disbelieving the evidence of his own ears.

'But...but...*I'm* Ronnie Westmacott!'

First published in *Suffolk Writes Anthology*, 2022

The Flight

The cabin lights dimmed as the two great engines roared into life. Erika pressed herself back into the solid comfort of the seat, her hands gripping the arm rests. Eyes closed as the front wheels lifted off the tarmac, she repeated the mantra she'd been taught and focused on her breathing. In two three, out two three, in two three, out two three. She opened her eyes just as the cabin lights came back on and allowed her body to relax. They were in the air. She was safe.

She opened the book she had bought in the duty-free shop and allowed herself a moment to savour the smell of the never read pages. Ordering a small bottle of over-priced wine from the steward, she settled back into the seat and allowed herself to fall back in time as she turned over page after page. It was the biography of a Lancaster bomber pilot, telling the story of his acts of heroism during the dark days of World War II.

The book was interesting, but the wine was having a soporific effect on her and she found her eyes closing involuntarily. Her head slipped sideways, crashing into the hard plastic of the cabin window, jerking her back to consciousness. A streak of unexpected colour outside the plane caught her eye and she peered into the half light of the sky that was all but obscured by the clouds. There it was again. Just a momentary flash, but a definite streak of green. She took another mouthful of wine and shook her head, wondering if she was seeing things. For a moment, the clouds parted just enough for her to see the shape of an aeroplane flying alongside them. She jerked back from the window, knocking her book to the floor. The other plane had been far too close for comfort. It couldn't have been a commercial flight though; even the briefest of glimpses had been enough to show that it was significantly smaller that the jet she was travelling in.

Bending down awkwardly to retrieve her book, Erika's eye was caught by the cover illustration. It showed the author as a young man, leaning against his Lancaster, his laughter caught and frozen in time. It couldn't have been. Could it? Sitting up slowly, Erika shivered as a cool draught played over the back of her neck. She turned to apologise to her fellow traveller for her wriggling around, then stopped mid-movement. Where only moments earlier had been a seat containing a red-haired woman there was now empty space. Well, she thought, not quite empty, just not filled with what it should be. The cabin was now occupied by young men in flying jackets, guns and an assortment of ammunition.

Erika closed her eyes and opened them again, hoping that somehow that would make everything revert to normal again. It didn't. The young man in the tail turned round.

'OK boys, we're coming over land now, call out those enemy fighters and watch out for those flak guns. It's going to get a bit bumpy from here on in.'

Suddenly, he caught sight of Erika, sitting behind him.

'Who the bloody hell are you? How did you get on the plane?'

Erika shrugged, not trusting her voice to work.

'Well whoever you are, I hope you brought a parachute.

We're heading for Berlin tonight, so if you're a journalist you might get more of a story than you bargained for. It's not exactly a milk run. Name's Bill if you're interested. Bill Wyatt. Tail gunner extraordinaire.' He flashed her a grin. 'First one they aim at usually, so you might want to move somewhere a bit safer. Not that anywhere's safe really, but she's a good girl – she's looked after us so far.'

'Bill Wyatt?'

'That's right. Why? Heard of me have you?' The grin widened.

'Not exactly. I don't reckon you need to worry too much though. I've got a feeling you'll be OK.'

She smiled back at him and closed her eyes, brushing away the tears that had suddenly sprung up. When she opened them again, it was to be greeted by the bright lights of the Ryanair cabin.

'We're beginning our descent into Berlin Schoenefeld airport now. Please return to your seats and ensure that they are in the upright position and all luggage is stowed in the overhead lockers or under the seat in front of you.'

This time, Erika didn't feel the usual sense of fear as the plane made its way down to the runway, even managing a small smile at her neighbour when a drop in air pressure made the plane bounce a little as they approached the final stage of their descent. She was still feeling a little dazed as she handed over her passport to the stern-looking man behind the bullet proof glass.

He slid her passport under the screen.

'Welcome to Berlin, Miss Wyatt. Hope you have an enjoyable stay.'

The Railway

Richard jogged steadily down the track, his breath hanging in clouds that puffed forth with every alternate strike of his feet. The old railway line, overgrown in many places and consequently less popular with other runners, was the perfect place for him to run out his frustration. Teenage children and a menopausal wife meant strained silences punctuated by violent quarrels, sudden squalls that sprang up from a calm sea then dissipated into a frenzy of sobbing. This was his safe harbour, his place of calm he shared with no-one.

The mist was coming down as he approached the disused station at the end of the line; it was a thin wet haze, clear enough to see through, but which brought with it the kind of insidious creeping cold that chilled you from the inside out, rising through the layers of flesh and clothing to re-join the air without.

A man appeared as if from nowhere, a pick clutched tightly in his hand, but Richard was past him before he could do more than mutter a quick 'hello' between exhalations.

'Odd,' he thought. The track was usually deserted, especially at twilight when the light was dropping to a softer, subtle shade of purple, clothing the unlit track in a gauzy veil.

He jogged on as far as the beginning of the platform, then looped a 360 to head home. The regular slap of his trainers on the wet path echoed around him and the occasional twitter of a nesting bird hung in the air, but of the man he had passed, there was no sign. The abandoned railway line was just that; there were no trails leading off it and no broken bushes to indicate anyone had forced their way through. Richard was completely alone.

The mist was becoming thicker now, obscuring all but the closest objects and these loomed out at him, the fading light throwing shadows in his path as the encroaching darkness folded itself around him. The soft twittering of the nesting birds had given way to the screeching of an owl and the feathery rush of its wings as it swooped low over his head, arrow straight and focused on the prey below it. Still no sign of the man and he was halfway to the main road now. Surely he should have overtaken him by now?

A branch cracked somewhere underfoot and he broke into a sprint, heart and feet pounding in unison.

First published on my website, 2020

Through The Glass Darkly

Why is he such a bastard?

It's a question Rachael asks herself on a regular basis. Maybe there's something wrong with her? Does she expect too much of him? Yes, that must be it. She's only a waitress, while Ben goes to the gym every day and has a high-pressure job. There's no wonder he doesn't have time to put the bins out or do the washing up. She needs to lower her expectations. She should be more like his mother who's Mary bloody Poppins. Practically Perfect in Every Way, she can do no wrong, so it's obviously Rachael's fault they don't get on.

'She raised me on her own, Rache, cut her some slack.'

Cut her some slack? Any slacker and she'll float away. Actually, come to think of it, that wouldn't be such a bad thing, would it? If she did, maybe they'd have a chance of being happy. *When Anna's not around to stir things up, Ben's so much nicer. Last weekend he even gave my credit cards back and allowed Mum and Dad to visit.* All that will stop the minute his mother returns though. There'll be a row – there always is – Anna will act hurt and Ben will take her side as always.

Mary Poppins? Cruella DeVil more like! Mind you, even Cruella got her just deserts in the end.

The thought makes Rachael smile and she scrubs at the tea stain on the counter, imagining she's rubbing away at the satisfied smirk that crosses Anna's face every time Ben takes her side. She longs for someone who'll look after her and treat her like a princess, wants someone to look at her like the man by the window looks at his wife. Part of her regular Wednesday crowd, she sees them most weeks and they've obviously been together a long time, but it's so clear he still adores his wife and Rachael doesn't want to settle for anything less for herself.

Across the cafe, George's fingers twist compulsively around the fringe of his new scarf. Suddenly uneasy, he hangs it neatly over the back of his chair. He bought it to complement his wife's favourite coat, wishing, even as he'd handed his card over, that he was brave enough to buy the red coat that would match hers. Fran's so beautiful she can wear anything and make it look good, but his father's lectures are so deeply engrained George has never been able to break free of them. His clothes are all sensible. Chosen to blend in.

'Don't try to stand out lad, it never ends well. Just keep your head down and the buggers'll leave you alone.'

His father was the first in his family to pass the 11+ and never quite felt he belonged amongst his middle-class peers. He'd never been able to lose his working-class tongue so adopted an odd way of speaking – an attempt to mimic the more cultured tones of his classmates – that marked him out more effectively than his natural voice would ever have done. As a result, he'd been determined his eldest son would not bear the same stigma.

'Don't give 'em any reason to notice you. Just try to fit in' was always the response to any fashionable clothing or creative urges. It crushed George slowly until he finally became a man who belonged, but not the man he wanted to be.

His younger brother Robert, or Robbie, as George supposes he should refer to him, had rebelled against their father's strictures and fled to London, where he'd gone off to do something creative. *What is it Robert does?* Something arty, he's sure. *Maybe to do with one of the big museums?* Robert's overdue a visit and George has thought about going up to London to see where his brother works, but the big city scares him: all those people rushing about with no heed for the traveller unfamiliar with the confusing layout of the Tube. And Robert always manages to find a way to irritate him. He has no idea how Robert's going to manage when he retires; any time George asks about his brother's pension plans, he's dismissed with an airy wave of the hand.

'I'll worry about that when the time comes. Pensions are for people who plan to give up work.'

His attitude is irresponsible, but then that's Robert all over; living for today without a thought for tomorrow. And yet, the very things about his brother that drive him wild with frustration, are exactly the things that drew him to Fran all those years ago. She'd been so wonderfully unspoilt and free of pretension. Even now, she gives him life through her own joy for living and hope that there's still time for him to - *what is it called these days?* - find himself. Fran will help him look. The red tartan scarf is just the first step. He gazes at her across the table, imagining her laughing gently at his new-found joie-de-vivre and a small smile tugs at the corners of his mouth, encouraging him to be bold and take hold of her hand.

When George's hand slides across hers, Fran's pretending to gaze out of the window, but is observing her husband of forty years out of the corner of her eye. In his black jumper and navy jeans he seems to merge with the scenery outside; the sky and pavement both a murky, indiscriminate colour. Similarly, his car, which - if she squints and tilts her head - she can just see parked outside, is dark grey and only adds to the sense of a muted world, as though they're all being subsumed into a soupy nothingness. Even the congealed beans that stick to his plate have been bleached of colour so they lie feebly glued together, pale reflections of themselves, the only remnants of George's sole act of rebellion against conformity; a cooked breakfast at lunchtime.

She'd like to travel now they've retired and has suggested visiting Mexico, Easter Island, Peru - all places she has a deep-rooted longing to see. Thanks to George's obsessive need to set a little aside each month 'just in case', they have the money to do it, but George doesn't trust the food or the sanitation. So, they continue to have their annual two weeks in a gîte in the Loire Valley, where Fran uses her schoolgirl French at every opportunity, just for the thrill of finding out if she can make herself understood.

'I don't know how you do it. I'd never have the courage.'

Well of course you wouldn't, George. When have you ever had the courage to do anything?

The bright but tasteful clothes, well-manicured nails and subtly dyed hair give her an appearance of sophistication, but beneath all the superficiality, she's still the awkward East End girl whose teachers told her she would never amount to anything. Forty years ago, George seemed the safe option, a step up the social ladder, but now she's bored.

It's not me, it's him.

How could she not have seen it before? How has it taken her decades to realise that her husband is quite possibly the most boring man she's ever met? His hand strokes the back of hers and she shivers. Even his new scarf annoys her. It's so out of touch with everything else he wears.

What on earth possessed him to buy something so lurid? He never usually wears anything brighter than bottle green.

She feels a scream rising up her throat, choking her.

It might have been different. He might have been different. If they'd had children. They'd tried. After a number of disappointments she'd been to the doctor, who'd told her it would be safer not to try for any more. She'd been willing to risk it, but George said no, he was content with just the two of them. But she wasn't. She isn't. Motherhood was always in her plans and she looks enviously, even now, at mothers with their young babies, often wondering how they can bear to just leave them to cry, or worse, ignore them completely. Not like the lovely girl across the aisle from them, who's been happily playing with her son since they sat down. *I'd give anything to swap seats.*

'Peek-a-boo. Peek-a-boo.'

Sodding bloody peek-a-boo. How long does it take to heat up a jar of baby food, for God's sake?

If she has to do this for much longer she's going to completely lose it.

'Yes darling, peek-a-boo. I know you're hungry, but you just need to wait a few more minutes.'

Please don't start screaming. Please.

She can cope with the endless game as long as it keeps the screaming at bay. She sees them all the time, those perfect mothers with their happy contented babies and wonders what their secret is. Why is it always her child who threatens the eardrums of anyone in a three-mile radius? What's she doing wrong?

'Where've you gone? Oh there you are!'

Maybe it's me. Maybe I'm not cut out to be a mother.

Her Mum always made it all sound so straightforward, but

then she'd breastfed both her children, so perhaps that was it. Breastfed babies are said to be more contented, but Jamie just hadn't taken to it. She'd tried her best, truly, even when she could have wept for the pain when he alternated between biting her and refusing to latch on, red-faced and screaming until he made himself sick all over her. Maybe she shouldn't have given up so quickly though. It was true he seemed happier with the bottle and she could at least feed him outside the house now without feeling as though everyone was staring at her.

What if he gets ill because he hasn't got the immunity from the breast milk? I'll never forgive myself if anything happens to him.

Oh no...she mustn't cry in public!

Hold it together Lucy. Where on earth is his food?

It would be so much easier if Rory was here; he always manages to calm him down. She'd give anything to be able to hand her son over to his Dad and just get some sleep – even five minutes would be enough – but Rory works such long hours it isn't fair to expect him to help out at home as well. Other mums all seem to be able to function on no sleep, so why can't she? Or maybe their babies sleep through the night. Jamie probably should be by now as well.

Is his routine wrong? Should he be put down earlier? Or later? Perhaps there's something wrong with him and that's why he won't sleep? This isn't how it's meant to be, I should be treasuring every moment. I should be happy to have him. I'm so lucky - lots of women can't have kids. I am happy, I'd just be happier to be asleep at the moment. I'm an awful person. What kind of mother isn't always grateful for their own child? The only thing I'm grateful for at the moment is that she's finally brought his food over. I could have got it quicker myself. It must be nice to have a job like this – lots of people to talk to, no responsibility and money at the end of the month. Maybe I should go back to work? But what about Jamie? Can I really let someone else look after him?

'Can I pay the bill, please?'

Rachael takes the money and smiles as she watches the couple leave the café. It's a dull, dark afternoon, typical of those depressing days that follow the brightly festive ones of Christmas, but his tartan scarf and her red coat make them visible, even as the rest of them is swallowed up by the encroaching mist. They look good together and she smiles. *One day…one day I'll have that too.*

First published in *A Cinque Port Collection*, 2022

A Passing Fancy

'It's just a passing fancy,' I told E. 'D has no interest in marriage. Not with me, not with anyone. He gets bored quickly. In a few months, I'll be pensioned off with a gift or two and we'll go back to our life as it was before.'

E shook his head. He didn't like it. Why would he? What man would be happy at the thought of sharing his wife with another. He saw the benefits of the relationship, but he didn't like the price he'd have to pay.

'You can't have both, honey. Ambition or love. Which is it to be?'

Of course, he picked ambition. And I don't blame him any more than I do myself. I'd have made the same choice in his shoes.

Everything went to plan at first. D was infatuated with me and I knew exactly what he needed. Mothering. Someone to think for him. Everything he didn't at home. There, everyone told him what to do without paying him the courtesy of letting him think it was his own idea. And as for mothering – that's a laugh. There was none of that. No one to tell him how clever he was or what wonderful company he could be. Just cold disapproval and the sense that nothing was ever good enough. He was always expected to be something more than he was. Except with me. I knew how to flatter him, how to cajole him into doing the things he hated.

'Come with me,' he'd say. 'I can get through it if I know you're waiting for me.'

'Oh darling you flatter me. You're strong enough to do anything. But I'll come if it will make you feel better.'

He buried his face in my neck, breathing hot kisses on my skin. I knew where we were headed and I gritted my teeth. Sex wasn't something I particularly enjoyed. It wasn't necessary to me in the same way it was to him, but it was the price I had to pay to keep my position.

He knew there'd be a terrific row when it all came out, so we had to be careful and when we went away, E always came with us. If my husband was one of the party, then there couldn't possibly be any impropriety. After all, what husband would turn a blind eye to something so blatant? It was inconceivable. Nevertheless, even we underestimated the force of the reaction when they found out. I begged him to let me go home, but he refused.

'I need you here.'

'I'm harming you by staying.'

'I'll harm myself if you leave.'

'Don't be ridiculous,' I told him. 'This is more than either of us bargained for. We have to end this now before it's too late.'

He gripped my arm and the expression on his face froze me. 'I won't give you up. Remember darling, I sleep with a gun under my pillow. One squeeze is all it would take. If you leave, that's what I'll do.'

I threw my arms around him and begged him not to speak

of it again. What else could I do? I couldn't have his death on my conscience. It would be like killing a child, for that's what he was. They don't like being told 'no' either.

I tried so many times to get him to see sense. I even left. Hid. He found me.

'When will you realise you can't hide from me? You can go wherever you want, but wherever you go I will follow you. I cannot live without you.'

He spoke to friends, colleagues, tried to get them to support us. Some did, most didn't. Most saw me for exactly what I am – a woman out for herself. They know my type. We've existed for hundreds of years performing the same function for different men. I'm no different to the others. Not really. However much, he might like to think otherwise.

Something changed in him during that time and that was when I realised I'd won. I was going to get my freedom back. I telephoned E and told him I would stop the divorce proceedings. There was no need to continue the charade. D had agreed that we were being ridiculous and the only course of action left was to give me up, to let me go back to E. For him to focus on his new job. I would only be a distraction.

'I thought maybe I'd go to Paris. Lose myself there for a while until all this blows over.'

'I have friends with an apartment in Cannes. Go there instead. It will be harder for them to find you. I'll let them know it's all over and then you can disappear. No one will bother you after that.'

I agreed. I didn't care anymore. I just wanted out. I was suffocating. D telephoned to let me know all was well and proceeding exactly as he'd planned. He didn't want to rehearse his speech with me, just told me how to listen in when he delivered it.

'I think you'll be proud of how clever I've been,' he said. 'Everything will be just fine, you'll see. When it's done, we'll both be free to live again without being followed at every turn. They'll be off our backs once it's all over.'

So here I am, sat alone in a borrowed apartment waiting to hear him give me back my freedom. My life. My husband. E is waiting in Paris for me. He asked to come here tonight so we could listen together, but I wanted to be alone. Even the servants have been sent away for the evening. I have few regrets, but hurting E so badly is one of the biggest. I never imagined things would go so far. I'm not blind – I can see in the mirror I'm not the kind of woman men lose their heads over – but D did. It's almost finished now though. We've nearly reached the end of the road and I'm glad. I didn't want any of this and I feel the excitement beginning to bubble within me at the thought of my reunion with E. It won't be long now.

I glance at my watch. It's time. I lean over and turn the wireless on. The static crackles for a moment and then I hear his voice.

'At long last I am able to say a few words of my own. I have never wanted to withhold anything, but until now it has not been constitutionally possible for me to speak.'

He pauses for breath. I anticipate the break in his voice as he solemnly declares he has made the choice to put his country before his heart. I pour myself a glass of champagne and let the words wash over me.

'But you must believe me when I tell you that I have found it impossible to carry the heavy burden of responsibility and to discharge my duties as King as I would wish to do without the help and support of the woman I love.'

This isn't what we agreed. Red spots drop onto my dress. The stem of my glass has snapped.

'And now, we all have a new King. I wish him and you, his

people, happiness and prosperity with all my heart. God bless you all! God save the King!

God save the King, I want to cry, *What about me? God save me!*

First published in *Makarelle*, 2022

Under The Hammer

Adrian sits in the car, feeling the engine thrumming through the seat. He needs to get out, but the programme on the radio catches his attention, distracting him from thoughts of the work he needs to tell the garage people about. He has bigger things than the car to worry about – his marriage for example – but he can only deal with one thing at once.

So many things have gone wrong with his car over the last few weeks and he lists them in his head, trying to engrain them into his memory: passenger window, cigarette lighter, bulb light, blowers. He repeats them to himself all the way across the forecourt and into the glass fronted building that serves as the reception area. He remembers learning Latin endings like this at school: i, isti, it, imus, istis, erunt; bam, bas, bat, bamus, batis, bant; o, s, t, mus, tis, nt. Of course, he no longer has any idea what they were the endings of but chanting them aloud had clearly chalked them into his brain forever.

By the time he's got to the desk and started to speak to the receptionist, the Latin endings have driven the car issues out of his brain and he has to count up the problems on his fingers in a bid to recall them. It's like that a lot at the moment, things that are important being lost at the expense of something so trivial. Years of love and affection have disappeared in a miasma of arguments about the washing up, the children, the bins, money. All the usual dramas of married life and yet somehow they have become so large, they now seem insurmountable and all he can ask is *how long do we have left?* He can think of little else beyond the ending of this relationship.

It comes as no surprise that he can't focus on the book he needs to read, being distracted by the episode of 'Everybody Loves Raymond' that is blaring out from the garage television. He only ever watches the show on occasions like this and he doesn't even particularly like it. Frustrated, he tries to return his focus to the book. Someone in the family is talking about relationships and Adrian scowls. He doesn't want to hear this now.

All around him, the noises of day to day life in a garage continue. *I've done my ankle in already; that's a great start to the day.* The phone rings incessantly. *Good morning, Hayes Garage. How may I help you?* Mechanics walk backwards and forwards across the tiled floor, boots squeaking and leaving a black trail to follow through to where the real work happens. *Am I meant to be doing all of these?* A child is playing with the handles on a bright red Mini and the sales attendant frowns, powerless to step in and take on the role of the parent. Adrian also frowns, wondering where the parent is and distracted once again by the ringing of the phone, turns his attention once again to the television, now showing 'Frasier'.

He's having sex with the station manager on her desk; Frasier that is, not Adrian. Adrian is just envious. They can't keep their hands off each other and although it makes for entertaining viewing, Adrian doesn't smile. Can't smile. Too painful. He can remember when he and Jason used to be like that. It feels like a lifetime ago now. When was the last time they had any kind of sex at all, let alone such a passionate encounter? He thinks he can recall a brief peck on the cheek a few days ago, a distracted kiss on Jason's way out of the door. Has it really been so long? On the TV, Niles is angry at his wife's selfishness, throwing priceless ornaments around his living room, finally expressing his repressed anger, much to the delight of his father and brother. Adrian wishes he could do the same, but he's not sure Jason would care. Would he even notice? *Well he never notices when the dishwasher needs emptying.* Adrian tries to force the snarky voice inside him to be quiet. The dishwasher is insignificant compared to the love they share. Isn't it?

The customer opposite gets up and changes the channel and Adrian feels a brief flare of annoyance at not being asked if he minds, before recognising that he is being irrational and unreasonable. After all, to all intents and purposes, he is reading, not watching the TV. *I should be used to it by now,* he reasons. After all he's ignored at home, blending in with the furnishings. Why should it be any different anywhere else?

It's 'Homes Under The Hammer' now with the annoyingly perky and overexcited presenter. Martin something or other, who clearly doesn't understand what stream of consciousness is. Why do these people insist on using terms incorrectly? Trying to sound clever never comes off the way you want it to, so what's the point? *Not like Jason,* he thinks, *he actually is that clever.* Adrian feels an irrational burst of pride in his husband, feeling the anger of that morning's exchange die away. He looks back at the TV where the dilapidated house Martin has just filmed is now being auctioned off. Where do the people on the programme get the money from to buy these houses? Who has 150k just sitting around in their bank account? Not to mention the cost of renovating the places. None of them look like millionaires, they all have ordinary jobs, so what's their secret?

"Ravi and Aruna have brought the bungalow back from the brink."

Is it that easy? Is it really possible to take something so close to destruction and renovate it to a sparkling new standard? Could he and Jason do that with their marriage? Would it really be as simple as just giving it a facelift? The foundations have been secure enough over the years, it's just looking a bit unloved and uncared for at the moment. Maybe a fresh coat of paint and some new wallpaper is all it really needs. Marks and Spencer, he thinks. Dine in for two, nice bottle of wine. See what happens. His phone vibrates and he glances down at the screen.

Sorry about this morning. Will sort it this evening. Hope car is ok. J x

First published in *Makarelle*, 2021

Dream A Little Dream Of Me

Elspeth gazed out of the window, idly stirring the rapidly cooling coffee in front of her. She sighed, trying to block out the thoughts that crowded into the already full space inside her head. Everyone was looking at her: the waitress was annoyed she hadn't ordered any food, the cleaner would be cross about the amount of water she was dripping onto the floor, the other occupants of the café were judging her bedraggled appearance. She shouldn't be here, there were things to be getting on with at home, the voices of her family accused her. *Stop it*, she pleaded. This was usually her quiet space and they were spoiling it.

The Naze was the only place where their voices didn't normally bother her. It was where she'd felt her grandfather was most at peace and it was a refuge: from her family, her insecurities and well, just life, she supposed. The youngest of three siblings and the only one with a job that was deemed expendable by her more high-flying relatives – her sister was a doctor, her brother a lawyer – it had been made clear to Elspeth, when their grandfather had been diagnosed with dementia, that her notice had to be given in at the library and the responsibility of caring for him would fall on her shoulders.

In many ways, she didn't mind. She loved her grandfather and he had enough money for her not to have to worry about the loss of income. Admittedly, when he'd given her sole power of attorney, her mother, brother and sister had made a fuss about not being involved. That had continued only until her grandfather's solicitor stepped in on his behalf and said unless they were going to be directly involved in his client's day to day care, or had reason to believe Elspeth was going to steal all his money, it was far more straightforward to have just one person controlling the money. If they accused her of being ready to steal his money, they would need to take on some of his care themselves, so the complaints stopped. Well, she thought ruefully, the snide remarks and the hints about things that were needed but couldn't be afforded continued, but those at least were not daily utterances and were delivered at a much lower volume.

Those who didn't know Elspeth's mother might have assumed – from her loud lamentations – that she would personally want to take care of her father, but Elspeth knew her mother's temperament would not allow for that. At the time of the diagnosis, Meredith Gardiner was in New York for work and such was the importance of her meetings, nothing could be allowed to interfere with them. Flying home was completely out of the question – she was a vital part of the company's team and as such, was stuck in the city for at least the next few months. She did however have full confidence in her youngest daughter's abilities and was sure she was absolutely the best person for the job. It was incredibly difficult being powerless to help her father, but she must do her best to soldier on under the troubling circumstances, as it was what he would want her to do. Of course, if Elspeth didn't feel she was up to the task of caring for her grandfather, they could always find a home for him to move into, but it would be awfully expensive. Not to mention it just didn't seem right to consign the care of one's relatives to complete strangers. *It's easy to think that when you can just delegate the care to your disappointing daughter.* Elspeth was cross with herself for even thinking it. Her mother did care, as did her siblings, but it was frustrating that she was always the one who had to deal with the practicalities of their expectations.

Elspeth duly rented out her little flat and moved into her grandfather's considerably larger house in Walton. At first, his illness had been relatively easy to manage, but as the disease's grip on his mind grew stronger, it became increasingly difficult to cope on her own and, feeling like a failure, she had been forced to reach out for help. Initially, she tried asking her siblings if either of them could assist her for a few hours a week, but her nieces and nephews all had clubs after school, which tied up her sister and her brother was in the process of having an extension added onto his house and needed to be at home to supervise the builders, who would take twice as long to complete the job if left to their own devices. Consequently, she was forced to ask the doctor if he could recommend any organisation that could help her out and to her surprise and relief, he put her in touch with people who came to her aid almost immediately.

During these periods of respite care, she came to the Naze to walk and clear her head. It reminded her of happier times when she'd brought her grandfather to walk around the Fossil Trail or to watch the birds as they dipped and darted across the scrubland. As walking became more difficult for him, they retreated to the café to watch the birds from inside and over endless cups of unfinished coffee and mountains of cake which never got eaten, Elspeth learned about the different species of birds that called the nature reserve home. When it became clear he no longer took the same pleasure in their visits, they stopped coming, but Elspeth returned alone, firstly in the few hours she spent away from the house and then again, weeks after his funeral, seeking the comfort of the familiar surroundings.

Today, it had been threatening rain from the moment she left the house and the sky had finally released the rain as she walked into the car park. In the short dash across the grass to the visitor's centre, she had been soaked, despite her waterproof coat and both she and it dripped steadily onto the floor below her chair.

Raising her mug to her lips and automatically blowing across it, Elspeth let her eyes drift around the crowded café. A man, easily as wet as she, but far better at carrying off the drowned rodent look, entered and made his way to the counter. Dark hair was plastered to his face and he wore the harassed look of someone who'd just had all their plans disrupted and had no reserve plan to fall back on. He looked over as he waited to collect his drink and caught her eye. Embarrassed to be caught staring, Elspeth flashed him a brief smile, then averted her eyes, returned her gaze to the gloomy view beyond the window and urged her mind to wander again. Her thoughts however, remained stubbornly fixed on the handsome stranger. He was extraordinarily good-looking, but just the sort of man she'd never dream of trying to catch the eye of. He was too far out of her league – even if she didn't recognise that herself, there had been enough shouts of laughter from her sister over the years whenever she expressed an interest in someone. But she could dream, couldn't she? Maybe he was the one who would finally appreciate her, who would recognise the worth in her that seemed invisible to everyone else.

'Excuse me? Is this seat taken?'

She turned to see the new arrival hovering expectantly by the chair opposite her.

'Not at all. Help yourself.' It wasn't a particularly imaginative response and was unlikely to dazzle him with its brilliance, but it was too much to expect her brain to come up with something witty and enticing when presented with the figure it had just been imagining a future with.

She expected him to move the chair to another table, but instead, he sat down, laying his sodden coat over the chair next to him.

'Thank-you,' he said, once he'd got himself settled. 'I wasn't expecting it to be so busy today. I guess the rain's driven everyone inside though. I had hoped to do some birdwatching, but I'm not dedicated enough to do it in the rain!'

'I suspect even the birds will have taken shelter from this.'

The rain was now coming down with such force that it was bouncing straight back up as though the tarmac was a trampoline and he nodded ruefully.

'You're probably right. Ah well. With any luck it'll stop soon. I'm Matt, by the way.'

'Elspeth.' She smiled again.

'Do you come here often?' he asked. 'I know most of the regulars by sight, but I don't remember seeing you around before, that's all.'

'I haven't been for a while, but I used to come a lot with my grandfather.'

To her surprise, she found herself telling him all about her grandfather's illness. It wasn't a story she shared easily with others, but he was somehow very comfortable to talk to.

'I'm sorry you've had such a hard time,' he said. 'It can't have been easy for you.'

'What about you?' Elspeth asked. 'What brings you here?'

'Escape.' He gave her a wry smile. 'I'm going through a messy divorce at the moment and it's a chance to step away from it all for a while.'

Elspeth's face twisted into a grimace.

'I'm so sorry,' she whispered. 'I didn't mean to pry.'

He held up a hand, protesting her apology.

'You didn't,' he assured her. 'It's nice to talk to someone without a vested interest to be honest. My wife, well ex-wife really, had an affair with my boss, so everyone has an opinion on it, whether I'm at home or at work.'

Instinctively, Elspeth reached out and covered his hand with her own.

'I'm so sorry,' she said again. 'I'm not surprised you need to escape for a while.'

'There's something very restful about this place, isn't there?'

'It certainly soothes the soul a little.'

He looked down to where her hand still rested lightly on his.

'I wonder… would it be too much to ask… do you think maybe we could rediscover it together? I know our situations aren't the same, but I've enjoyed talking to you today. The rain's eased off a bit – perhaps we could fit in a quick walk round the Fossil Trail before we have to leave?'

'That would be lovely,' Elspeth said, a faint blush tingeing her pale cheeks.

'Wonderful,' he said. 'I won't be a minute.'

Getting up, he hurried off in the direction of the toilets. Elspeth returned her gaze to the window, surprised to see that the rain was just as heavy as when she'd arrived.

She was startled out of her reverie by the sound of someone clearing their throat.

'Sorry. I could see you were miles away and I didn't want to make you jump.'

The man grinned sheepishly as a trickle of water dripped onto the table from the dark hair plastered to his face. Elspeth stared at him, too clouded in confusion to speak for a moment.

'I just wondered if it would be okay for me to join you?' he continued. 'It's just that it's a bit busier than I'd expected and there are no other seats.'

Elspeth nodded.

'Please. Feel free. It is a bit full, isn't it? I suppose the rain caught everyone unawares.' Taking a deep breath, she extended her hand.

'I'm Ellie.'

He grasped her hand and shook it firmly.

'Matthew. Nice to meet you.'

Tweeting Jolene

@flamehairedsiren wot is ur problem? Get ur own man & leave mine alone

@desparatedoll who is this?

@flamehaired siren don't pretend u don't know. How many men have you got?

@desperatedoll OMG it's you again, isn't it? How many times do I have to tell you I'm not sleeping with ur husband?

@flamehairedsiren then why is he talking about you in his sleep?

@desperatedoll IDK! We've only met a couple of times @ work

@flamehairedsiren When you look like you that's all it takes. You're beautiful.

@desperatedoll You really think so?

@flamehairedsiren Obvs! Auburn hair, ivory skin, eyes like emeralds. He says ur voice is like summer rain too.

@desperatedoll WTH does that even mean?

@flamehairedsiren IDK but whatever it is, he loves it. I'm begging u, pls don't take him away

@desperatedoll M8 it sounds like u cld do sooooo much better

@flamehairedsiren but I love him. I need him to be happy. If he leaves I'll just die.

@desperatedoll girl, you don't need no man to make u happy. Come out with me & I'll show u wot I mean

@flamehairedsiren I don't think he'd like that. He gets jealous.

@desperatedoll let me get this str8. He's talking about me in his sleep, but u aren't allowed a night out w/out him?

@flamehairedgirl you no wot? Ur right. We should totally go out.

@desperatedoll attagirl! Ditch the extra baggage and come have fun

@flamehairedgirl starting 2 see y he fancies u. DM me the details & it's a date.

@desperatedoll m8 you're pretty hot urself. Ur guy's an idiot. Let's show him wot he's missing. Don't w8. We're in a bar now.

@flamehairedgirl I'm up 4 that. Where 4 u?

@desperatedoll Barney's on Main Street

@flamehairedsiren Be there in 1/2hr. C U.

@desperatedoll drink will b waiting

First published in *Makarelle*, 2021 as Elizabeth Eastwood

Tarosvan or 'The Legend of Logres'

'Are we nearly there yet?'

I groaned. Arthur was awake.

'No, sweetheart.'

'How much longer will it take?'

'Would you like a bacon sandwich?' My husband interrupted and I smiled gratefully at him.

The offer was accepted, peaceful silence settled over the back of the car again and I resumed listening to Bill Bryson's *Notes From A Small Island*. This was exactly why we'd set the alarm for 3am and begun the long trek down to Cornwall at 4 o'clock in the morning. We were well over half way and our youngest son had only just woken up. I calculated that once he'd eaten the sandwich, we'd have a maximum of ninety minutes of him and Henry squabbling. You'd think that at sixteen and almost six there'd be enough of a gap for long car journeys not to descend into 'stop poking me', 'keep it on your side of the car' and my personal favourite, 'Muuuuuummmmm, can you have a word.' However, if you did, you'd be wrong! Most of our family holidays begin in this way and so we've learnt over the years that if we set off in the middle of the night, we stand at least half a chance of getting there without James and I needing to reach for the gin bottle the moment we arrive!

This year, however, was going to be a holiday with a difference. A month earlier we'd completed on our holiday flat and this was the first time we were going to make use of it. I'd spent the last month driving between North Essex and Cornwall every week, taking deliveries, assembling furniture, cleaning and generally getting the flat ready so that we could actually use it over the summer. Doing that whilst still trying to ensure that everything ran smoothly at home had been 'interesting' to say the least and I was ready for a break.

We decided that if we were going to make the most of both the flat and the area, we needed to learn more about Cornwall and its history. James and I both love the county and would love to move there eventually and we felt strongly that we needed to have as much of a sense of Cornish heritage as we could. Although it is part of England, there is also a feeling of separateness about it. It has its own language for a start, although we were both surprised and alarmed to discover that there are less than a thousand people who are fluent in Cornish and only a few thousand more who could have a basic conversation, or know the odd word. However, when you consider that the last person who claimed Cornish as their first language is traditionally believed to have died in 1777, perhaps it is more astounding that it has survived at all and is now a growing language. James decided he was going to add to the numbers, bought himself a book, downloaded an app and started learning basic words and phrases. I took on the task of learning about the history and folklore of Cornwall and this is where the twisted tales come in.

Until quite recently, whenever I thought of Cornwall in literary terms, it was usually romantic comedies set in quaint Cornish villages, Winston Graham's *Poldark* or Susan Cooper's *Over Sea Under Stone* and *Greenwitch*. I'd read *Rebecca* years ago but had no idea it was based on a real house in Cornwall. I stumbled across *Jamaica Inn* by accident when I was looking for an audiobook set in the county – I did a virtual walk from Land's End to John O'Groats and listened to books set in the counties I was walking through – and fell in love with it straight away. The haunting opening lines so perfectly captured both the scene and the essence of the book that I knew immediately this was an author whose writing I was going to adore.

However, it seems that romantic as Cornwall is portrayed – and it truly is – its real literary heritage may lie in the slightly less prosaic ghost story. There are literally hundreds of these things, as I discovered when I bought Michael Williams' *Ghosts Around Bodmin Moor*.

'Did you know Jamaica Inn is meant to be haunted?' James was reading leaflets in preparation for the 'flat folder' we were putting together for when family and friends used it.

'Pretty much everywhere in Cornwall seems to be haunted,' I said, waving *Ghosts Around Bodmin Moor* at him. 'And yes, everyone knows Jamaica Inn is haunted.'

'Well I didn't,' he said, looking a little put out.

'It was on *Most Haunted* years ago. We should watch it.'

'I don't like scary things, Mum.' Henry suddenly took an interest in the conversation.

I smiled at him. 'It'll be fine, honestly. Come on, it'll be fun.'

He looked doubtful, but I found the episode on YouTube and we settled down to watch it. It was hard to take it seriously when the mediums generally just repeated the stories we'd already been told but with a few added embellishments. None of us completely dismiss the idea of ghosts, but it wasn't massively convincing. The only bit that was a little bit spooky was when they were in the boiler room and that was destroyed for us by the very northern accented exclamation of, 'Something touched me side!' before they all sprinted for the exit. The boys have always taken the mickey out of me for being northern and this became the catchphrase every time we went to Jamaica Inn for a drink. Someone would get poked and have to exclaim, 'Something touched me side' in an exaggerated northern accent so we could all fall about laughing and pretend that we weren't a little bit spooked by the fact we were in a place with such a ghostly reputation.

'You know they do ghost hunting nights here?' I said.

Henry nodded. 'I like the idea, but I think I'd probably be heading for the door as soon as there was a noise!'

Towards the end of the holiday, we decided to take a hike up Roughtor – a mere 400m climb over rocks to the top.

'Why this walk?' James asked.

'What do you mean?' I frowned, puzzled.

'All your walk suggestions have an ulterior motive. There's always something you want to see, or a story you want to be at the location of. What's this one?'

In fairness, he was perfectly correct. I dragged the family across Fylingdale Moor in pursuit of Dracula, we climbed up a huge hill in Bath because I wanted to walk in the footsteps of Catherine Morland and Henry Tilney, we'd visited Jamaica Inn more times than I could count simply because of Daphne Du Maurier and the last time we'd been in Cornwall I took them all on a very muddy route march around Frenchman's Creek in search of La Mouette and her captain. Henry has still to forgive me for the loss of his Skechers in the mud on that walk! Roughtor was no exception. At the base of the Tor is the memorial to Charlotte Dymond, probably one of the most famous of Cornwall's ghosts.

The eighteen-year-old Charlotte was murdered near Roughtor Ford in 1844, allegedly by her lover, Matthew Weeks. He was arrested and hanged for her murder. His conviction seems to have rested largely on his written confession. However, there is some doubt about whether or not it was actually written by him. Local people were outraged by this vicious attack on a young girl and collected the funds to raise a memorial to her, which still stands near to where she was found. The day of our walk was beautifully sunny with lots of people around. We saw the memorial, but couldn't get near it as it was fenced off. It was hard to imagine such a brutal act taking place in this stunning location – whether Weeks was guilty or not, someone slit Charlotte's throat that day – but I would imagine that in winter, at night, the moor might take on a different feel and Charlotte's ghost is still said to walk the ground where she was murdered. The impact of this tragic tale is still felt today – as recently as 2015 locals raised money to buy a headstone for her and the trial of Matthew Weeks is one of the star attractions at Bodmin Jail, where visitors get to vote on his guilt.

Over the holidays, we had several more encounters with supernatural – or at least with stories of it – including at The Cathedral of the Moor in Altarnun. I'd wandered away from the boys to have a look at the graves and ended up inside the church on my own. I've been in a lot of empty churches over the years and generally they're quite peaceful places. In this one however, I definitely felt the weight of history pressing down. I had the distinct feeling that it was waiting for something and although I wasn't aware that the church was haunted – I thought the ghost was in the old rectory which we'd yet to locate – there were patches of the church that felt much colder and when I stood at the back I felt decidedly odd – as though both the church and I were waiting for something to happen. It's not a feeling I've often had before. The sunlight outside was a welcome relief and I was greeted there by an incredibly friendly local who took me round the churchyard and pointed out the graves of the vicar and his servant, who she told me are said to haunt both churchyard and old rectory. Her son, who like her is a sceptic, once told her he'd seen a figure in the doorway when he'd been on his own in the church, not far from where I'd felt the cold. I'm still not convinced, but it was an uneasy feeling to hear the coincidence in the location.

The most interesting thing for me about all these ghost stories, is that in the summer holidays I always know I'm not going to get any writing done. It's just too difficult to find the quiet time I need when all three of my boys are at home and wanting my attention. This summer, although I didn't get any actual writing done, I did make copious notes about ideas for new stories and novels based in Cornwall and using many of the ghostly tales I'd read about as a starting point. I reckon I've probably got enough for a collection of short stories and at least three novels, which should keep me going for a while! All I need now is to find the time to write them all, which reminds me of a conversation James and I had on the car journey home at the end of the summer.

'I've managed to sign Arthur up for Kid's Club, so if we need to use them before or after school now, we can.'

'That's good,' he replied absently. 'Does that mean we'll be okay for when you go on the writing retreat in March?'

'Yes.' I paused a moment. 'Of course... you do realise it also means that if I want to have a few days to crack on with some writing in peace, I can book him into it and go down to the flat on my own and have my own mini retreat.'

Out of the corner of my eye, I swear I saw his skin go a shade paler and a slight sheen of perspiration cover his face.

'Erm... are you planning to do that soon then?'

'Not really, it was just a thought. Why?'

'Arthur.'

The boy in question piped up from the back of the car. 'You said my name. Did you want me?

'No, darling. You carry on watching your film.
'OK. Are we nearly there yet?'

Bibliography
Williams, Michael *Ghosts Around Bodmin Moor*, Bossinney Books
http://www.cornwalladvertisers.co.uk/article.cfm?id=105263&headline=Charlotte+Dymond+finally+gets+a+headstone&sectionIs=news&searchyear=2017
https://www.reddit.com/r/CornishLanguage/comments/lut93n/how_many_people_speak_cornish_fluently_in_2021/

First published in *Makarelle*, 2021

Wait For No Man

I watch the ripples on the surface of the lake as they're carried along by the soft spring breeze and I feel sorry for them. I know what it's like to be pulled along by a force that's stronger than you, that gives you no say in where you go or what you do. I've felt the helplessness of being dragged along by an undercurrent too strong for you to fight against.

I suppose that's how I ended up here, sitting on the newly mown grass at the side of the campus lake watching my fellow students - most of whom are half my age - while trying to ignore the burrito bus and the smell of its wares wafting across the water. At forty, middle age is encroaching on my once trim waist and I engage in a daily battle with it, in an attempt to keep the war at a stalemate. On a normal day, I'd have been first in the queue. Today, the smell turns my stomach and I consider moving upwind of the red double decker. I feel sick. Experience tells me I'm not actually going to be sick, but this nausea hits like the incessant thumping bass from a nightclub speaker after one too many gins.

It's entirely my own fault of course. It always is. If I'd been polite and disinterested, or even just honest, I wouldn't be sitting here like this, so I probably don't deserve any sympathy and that's okay I'm used to that too.

The trees around the lake dance to the rhythm of the wind, bent and burdened by the weight of their cherry pink wigs. I have to tell him. Embarrassment is no longer an excuse; I can't really claim to be embarrassed with someone who's seen me naked, can I?

Being by the water wondering how my life has got to this point is all too familiar and I find myself thinking about those other occasions. Could I have done things differently? I don't know. Maybe.

It had been a shock to discover life was not like my stories, with a sense of structure that carried you through to the end. It was more like the sea in the midst of a storm - wild, unpredictable, out of control, terrifying you with its strength of will. I'd thought I was lucky. He'd done...what was it called in those days? The honourable thing. There was nothing honourable about it, although to give him credit, he never blamed me after. He just accepted life as it was and we drifted along, but the damage was done; marriage had put paid to my plans to go to university.

That was, until three years ago. With my fortieth birthday looming on a horizon that grew frighteningly nearer with each passing day, I began to wonder where the last two decades had gone. I was still in the same house I'd moved into at eighteen, less crowded since the death of Ian's parents, but still just as stultifying. The constant ticking of the clocks with which Ian's mother had filled every available surface and the doleful dong of the grandfather clock in the hallway marked out every second of my day. Seconds in which nothing happened, minutes I spent staring at the beige monotony of the shag pile carpet, hours I spent alone not knowing or caring where Ian was, until eventually I could bear it no more. I had to know if she was still there – the eighteen year old me – the me who loved life, who enjoyed the challenge of making words work for me.

I filled in the application form in a frenzy, submitting it before I could be convinced not to. When the acceptance letter arrived I kept it secret for months, unable to face the ridicule I felt sure would follow it, until one day I left it on the kitchen table when I went to do the shopping. It had been moved when I returned, but to my relief nothing was said and in September, I merely left the house to attend lectures instead of the local supermarket

* * *

'Is anyone sitting here?'

Two beautiful brown eyes smiled at me over the top of the dividing wall between our desks.

'I don't think so.' I returned the smile politely and went back to my editing.

A pen landed on the floor by my feet and I picked it up to return it, receiving a dazzling smile in thanks. A few more minutes ticked by and a tapping on the other side of the partition pulled me out of my thoughts again.

'Sorry,' he whispered, as I glared at the only part of him I could see.

After he'd stretched his legs out and kicked me for the third time, I gave up any hope of finalising my edits. The deadline was at noon so my tutor would just have to have it in its current state. I was packing up to leave when a book landed in the same spot as the pen before it. Sighing, I stooped and returned it to its owner.

'Sorry,' he grinned, eyes twinkling. 'Let me buy you a coffee to make up for disturbing you? I'm Joe, by the way.'

He looked so childlike standing there, a sheepish look on a face unmarred by worry or age lines, that I couldn't help but agree. *It's only coffee. He's half your age. It doesn't mean anything. You're not even attracted to him.* Besides, Ian wasn't taking the boat out until this evening and it was a better prospect than going home to complaints about lunch not being on the table when he got out of bed. *I can always claim that my lecture over-ran and I missed the bus. He probably won't care, but at least I'll have an excuse ready.* I briefly contemplated the idea of telling him what I'd really been doing. If I'd actually cared what he thought I might even have done it.

'Are you always this clumsy?' I asked.

Joe had the good grace to flush.

'I was trying to get your attention,' he said. 'I mean, I know it's probably not allowed, you being a lecturer, but I figured...well, you're not **my** lecturer, are you?'

But I was. With that simple compliment I was his. I couldn't remember the last time anyone had paid me one and that was all it took. I didn't correct his mistake; middle age was staring me in the face, berating me for a wasted life and this... this **boy** had made excuses in order to ask **me** out. Me! I probably had knickers older than him! I made a sudden decision to buy some new ones.

* * *

'I don't want to lose you.'

'We've been through this, Ian. I'm only going to uni. I'll be home in the holidays.'

'You'll forget all about me once you're there.'

It was like talking to a petulant child, but he was right. At 18, I'd already outgrown him and we both knew it. University would be the end of us and I was glad. Like Anne, I needed something more than Avonlea, but time had stood still for Ian; I knew he still expected to be greeted by shiny-faced beribboned children on his return home from work; dinner on the table and an adoring wife ready to listen to his tales of derring-do on the boat. '*You just don't understand how dangerous it is, Em. The North Sea is a cruel mistress. I could die at any moment!*' (I couldn't bring myself to worry overly; skate fishing off Clacton hardly compared to the wild seas off north-eastern Scotland after all.) He viewed with suspicion anyone who didn't fit his mould - Margaret Thatcher was a dangerous precedent and even in entertainment, women like Melanie Griffiths' 'Working Girl' were setting bad examples for impressionable young women.

* * *

'Was that OK?'

'It was fine.'

I stroked the smooth cheek that nestled into my shoulder. How could I tell Joe I only had one experience with which to compare him? It had been more than the span of his life since any man had touched me. How could I explain that his touch had made me feel complete again; I'd found the girl I'd been looking for.

* * *

It never occurred to me to think it odd when, on learning I was pregnant, Ian's first reaction had been neither shock nor disbelief.

'I s'pose this means no university then, but don't worry love, maybe you could do a course once the kids are at school.'

A few weeks later, in the lead up to the wedding, I'd fled from all the talk of hymns and seating plans. I cared little for one and less for the other - I'd dreamed of writing novels not orders of service. I could see the rest of my life stretching endlessly out before me, one long jumbled mess of bland dinners with relatives, sandcastles on the local beach with screaming children and small talk over cheap sherry and I couldn't breathe. Life was racing away from me. I was being left behind. Meg, Ian's cousin and my reluctant choice for chief bridesmaid, caught up with me just as I reached the end of the pier.

'It'll be OK, Em, you'll see. Nobody cares enough about **me** to get me pregnant just so's he can marry me.' She sighed, her fat bottom lip wobbling with self-pity.

In my annoyance at her use of the abbreviated name I hated, I nearly missed what she'd said. I couldn't even be sure I'd heard her correctly over the roar of the sea as it thundered against the iron legs of the pier.

'What do you mean?'

'Oh dear.' She giggled. 'Have I put my foot in it? I thought he must've told you by now. Ian sabotaged the condom. I think it's dead romantic,' she added quickly. 'He must love you an awful lot.'

For a brief moment I considered throwing myself, or her, over the railings, but I lacked the courage to follow through on the thought. Instead, I bent over the side, the cold metal barrier digging into the soft folds of my stomach. A feeling of nausea that had nothing to do with my condition rose inside me and the spray from the sea mingled with my tears. The only clear thought in my head was that he would never touch me again. My marriage was over even before the ceremony had begun.

When the bleeding started a few weeks later it was already too late. The ring on my finger bore angry witness to that fact and over the years it grew heavier until it became nothing more than the last link in a weighted chain that tied me to the village. I had responsibilities; ageing parents to look after, committees to sit on, events to organise, but my anger grew in tandem with that weight. Time had been taken from me and I had been robbed of the future that should have been mine.

*　*　*

I sense him coming before I see him, his long legs eating up the space between us as he strides across the grass, a lop-sided smile of greeting on his face. My courage is slithering under the surface of the lake, slipping away with every step he takes. My stomach flutters and I pass my hand across it, a gentle motion that soothes it.

All the moisture in my mouth has migrated to my palms and my usual command of words has abandoned me. How do I begin? Which secret should I tell first? Suddenly, I realise it doesn't matter. There's nothing to tie me here after the exams. And then there it is – a single moment of clarity. *I don't **need** anyone. I can do **all** of this on my own if I have to. I've been on my own for twenty years and I've survived. I've finally caught up with life and time is no longer my enemy.*

I trail my fingers in the water, watching the waves move in concentric circles. **I** am controlling the direction. **I** am in charge. I smile.

'We need to talk,' I say.

First published in *Suffolk Writes Anthology,* 2022

Who Parents The Parents?

'My turn CH-O-P, chop. Your turn.'

'CH-O-P, chop.'

'My turn, SH-I-P, ship. Your turn.'

'SH-I-P, ship.'

'My turn F-U-CK, fuck. O-FF, off.'

This last was inside Nina's head rather than on the home-learning video her five year old daughter was watching. She wondered if the teachers were ever tempted to say this as they had their clothes tugged by sticky hands and listened to the incessant whining of the children in their class. She didn't know how they did it. She could barely cope with one five year old, let alone thirty of the little darlings.

Her husband ambled past on his way to the fridge.

'You're doing so well darling. Very good,' he said.

'Patronising bastard,' Nina thought, before realising he was probably talking to their daughter rather than her.

'Could you do this with her for a little bit so I can get a shower?' she called through the open kitchen door.

'Sorry darling,' he said, 'I've got another meeting in twenty minutes.'

'That's okay,' Nina said. 'I can be quick.'
'But I wanted to make a cup of tea to have in the meeting.'
Nina gritted her teeth.
'You still can. I won't be long.'
She pushed her chair away from the table and pointed at the laptop screen.
'Her work's all there on the website.'

Inside the bathroom Nina turned the shower on then took a deep breath and leaned her head against the door for a moment, fighting against the threatening tears. *Why is it always me that has to give? Why is my work less important than his?* She knew why: money. It still wasn't fair though. Lucy was a good kid, but she needed constant supervision to get through the work. If they didn't do it, the school would be on to them, checking everything was ok. They'd done that the first week.

'Everything's fine,' Nina lied when Mrs Edwards rang. 'Lucy's had such fun, I just forgot to upload the pictures, that's all.

The reality of that first week was Lucy sobbing because she couldn't see her friends and her teacher, while Nina tried to be a caring parent at the same time as having a Zoom meeting with her boss, while her silenced mobile buzzed with angry texts from Steven hiding upstairs in the study. *Can you get her to stop that infernal wailing. I'm trying to write a report and I can't concentrate.* What the fuck did he think she was trying to do? She'd noticed she swore a lot more nowadays but reassured herself it was only in her head until yesterday when Lucy had knocked her drink over and shouted, 'Shit' at full volume while Steven was on the phone to a client.

There was a knock on the bathroom door.

'Nina? I can't work out what she's meant to do and my meeting starts soon.'

Nina looked in the mirror. A blurry smudge peered back

at her through the mist. She felt more like her reflection than a real person: slightly out of focus, smeared around the edges and somehow not quite there. She'd been completely consumed by Home-Schooling Mum. Nina the person no longer existed. Nina wondered if she ever really had. Was there more to her than mum, wife, cook, cleaner? She thought there might have been once. She touched the face in the mirror and a single droplet slid down the glass from the corner of its eye.

Steven knocked on the door again.

'Nina, seriously! I've got a meeting. Hurry up!'

The shower would have to wait. She could feel herself unravelling, patience and sense of self unspooling in tandem. Time was running out for the person she used to be and there was nowhere to run. She sank to the floor, hands over her ears while Steven pounded on the other side of the door.

'Nina. Nina? Nina!'

First published in *Makarelle,* 2021

Christmas Eve

My daughter has always loved Christmas. I'm flying out to spend it with her family and even I feel a tingle of excitement. The airport is packed, but I'm in luck and I spy a single unoccupied space.

As I sit down, the man in the next seat glances up. I see a spark of recognition in his eyes, but it flickers and dies and he returns his gaze to his book. I notice it's in German.

The velvet tones of Nat King Cole come through the speaker and I am whisked back to another Christmas Eve when I was young and still naïve enough to think it would be over soon.

* * *

The ball comes flying through the air. Instinctively I duck. Then I remember. It's OK. I rise up and meet it, the hard leather smacking off the side of my head. I have no idea where it's gone until a loud cheer erupts. Khaki-clad bodies bear me to the ground. Celebratory for once, not protective. They win in the end but the score doesn't matter. We exchange chocolates, cigarettes, season's greetings. Broken English. Even more broken German.

Stille nacht, heilige nacht. A lone voice begins then we all join in. *Schlaf in himmlischer Ruh.* Sleep in heavenly peace.

I haven't slept peacefully since that day.

* * *

The man raises his eyes again.

'It is you?' he asks. 'You score goal?'

I nod.

'We sang.' He gestures towards the speaker. 'You remember?'

'I remember everything.'

He puts his wrinkled hand over mine. 'Ich auch. Ich auch.'

We lapse back into silence, lost in thoughts of faces we once knew. My flight is announced and I turn to say goodbye to my comrade in arms, but his seat is empty.

Only the scent of cigarette smoke lingers.

The Yellow Lily

Linda took one last look around reception. Light bounced off the chrome and glass, lifting the smart grey interior and lending it an extra air of elegance. She smiled, satisfied. Her employees in their deep purple uniforms stood at the doors to their individual suites, ready to welcome Conquiesco's first customers of the day. Behind the closed doors, tattoo guns, aromatherapy oils, gel polishes and beautifully scented shampoos lay waiting to be called into service.

A slight frown twitched at the corner of Linda's eye and she forced down her rising anger. Josie's face was too heavily made up again. It was happening more and more often and something needed to be done about it. Maybe she could speak to Steve. Josie was one of their own after all. She was sure he'd be happy to have a word in the right ear.

Pushing that problem aside for a later time, she clicked across the tiled floor and unlocked the doors. Swiftly and with minimal fuss, she checked each client in and directed them to the correct person. Murmured greetings soon disappeared behind closed doors and silence once again descended over her domain. Only then did she allow her thoughts to return to the problem of Josie. She was a good girl and a hard worker – her nail designs were the most highly sought after in the city – but there were standards to be maintained. 'Conquiesco' had to come above all other considerations. She'd sacrificed too much to allow the business to fail. She tapped a 'Rouge Rite' coated fingernail on the desk. The familiar technique worked and she felt the usual sense of calm rise up through her body. Yes, something definitely had to be done about Josie.

The girl herself appeared to farewell her client and Linda beckoned her over. She waited until the woman had tapped her credit card on the machine and made another appointment before she acknowledged her anxious employee.

'We've been a little heavy with the foundation again this morning, Josie dear, haven't we? What is our make-up mantra?'

'Keep it neat and be discreet.' Josie's head hung low. 'I'm sorry, Miss Linda, I –'

'Head up dear, we talk to faces not shoes.'

Josie raised her head but twisted her face away. Linda stretched out a hand and gently turned the chin towards her. Her jaw tightened and the fingers of her free hand clenched into a fist.

'What was it this time? Caught it on the cupboard door, did we?'

'Yes. No. I mean...' Josie's miserable expression made Linda's breath catch in her throat. 'I opened the cupboard and a tin fell on me.' The words came out in a rush and she exhaled sharply.

'I see.'

'Please, Miss Linda... I know you've had to warn me before, but... I can't lose this job...'

Linda patted her hand.

'Now, now,' she said briskly. 'There's no danger of that.'

The outer door swung open and Linda waved Josie back to her suite, then turned to greet the new arrival.

'Good morning, Madam. How can I help you?'

'I'd like a tattoo.'

Linda's eyebrows rose. The woman in front of her was the most exquisitely turned-out creature she'd ever seen. Firmly middle aged and definitely part of the twinset and pearls brigade that haunted the rotary club dinners, she certainly fitted the description of Conquiesco's usual clientele. However, Linda would have expected to find her at the manicure table not under the tattoo gun. Steve, her supervisor, kept all his eyes firmly fixed on the people who worked in the building (the third eye, which was tattooed in the middle of his forehead always slightly disconcerted Linda) and Linda knew he'd be intrigued by this new client. Steve was an excellent tattooist in his own right – he was responsible for the beautiful blueberry that lay beneath the strap of Linda's Cartier watch. However, his main role was to deal with the other side of Conquiesco's business. The side that stayed hidden beneath the refined and elegant facade. He had a separate client list and his suite had a separate entrance to the rest of the business. It turned over a good profit but most of the time Linda liked to pretend she didn't know it existed.

'Lovely. Did you have something particular in mind, Mrs... Miss...?'

'Armstrong-Jones. Mrs Armstrong-Jones.' Mrs Armstrong-Jones shook her head. 'No idea at all, I'm afraid.' She looked around and lowered her voice. 'I don't even particularly like tattoos. I'm only getting one as revenge.'

Linda remained quiet. Experience had taught her that interrupting the confession often ended it. It had also taught her that an opening of this nature often led to the client being referred to Steve for a further consultation.

'It's my husband, you see. He hates them with a passion.

When our daughter got one last year he threatened to throw her out of the house. I found out he's been having an affair, so I'd like a tattoo of something that means 'I know'. That way, when he asks what on earth I think I'm playing at, I can just tell him what it means and watch his face as he realises I know all about the little slut he's keeping in a flat in St. James' Square.'

Linda nodded sympathetically, ignoring the slip in both language and accent. Mrs Armstrong-Jones had clearly not been born to the life she was leading and was desperate to cling onto it. Linda admired her tactics though. 'Don't be sad, be smart' was another of her little mantras. That one had seen her through her own husband's infidelity.

Reginald had been one of those men who always had to have his own way in everything. When they'd met, Linda had been a beautician, but he'd insisted that she gave up work when they got married. She'd been happy to turn her back on her old life. Her family was... complicated. Too well-known in the city. With her surname she hadn't a chance. She'd tried to distance herself from them even before meeting Reginald and he'd seemed the perfect solution. He had money, he had status and he loved her. Or so she thought.

He kept her at home and wheeled her out now and again for work purposes. She always had to be immaculately turned out in case he unexpectedly brought colleagues home for drinks. He got so cross if she wasn't prepared for them. At first, it had been a relief when he spent more and more time away from home. He'd told her he was going to the gym after work. The doctor had warned him there was a problem with his heart and he needed to lose some weight before he could have surgery. She'd encouraged him to go, pleased he was taking care of himself. Then she realised why. In Reginald's case, the flat had been on the Royal Crescent. He laughed when she confronted him over dinner. He was still laughing when she served him the blueberry pavlova she'd made specially for him. He stopped laughing when the deadly nightshade berries did their magic.

Of course, his widow had been thoroughly bewildered by the flat he was paying for. Did she wish to continue paying the rent on it? No, she didn't think so. Whatever he'd been using it for, it was surplus to requirements now. The money from his life insurance had paid for her to do various courses, including one in fine art. Then she'd bought Conquiesco and paid others to carry out the work needed to bring her visions to life. She only employed the very best of each profession and took pride in the knowledge there were people queueing both to be clients and employees of her establishment. It became common knowledge in the local community that the people who worked for Linda were treated like family. Her rules were strict and enforced, but any problems and they knew she could be relied upon to help.

Similarly, with the business, Linda quickly established a reputation for excellence. Nothing happened in Conquiesco without her approval: she designed each tattoo personally, she advised on new hairstyles, she was an expert in matching clients to colours which suited them. Nothing was beneath her notice. The best in the business did nothing more than carry out her instructions and she revelled in it. Where Conquiesco led, the rest of Bath soon followed.

'Where were you thinking of having the tattoo?' She asked.

Mrs Armstrong-Jones considered for a moment. She tapped the inside of her thigh. 'He likes to... you know...' she whispered. 'It will be the perfect time for him to see it.'

'In that case, how about an iris?' Linda said. 'They symbolise knowledge. They're quite tall flowers, so it would work well, I think.'

She sketched out the delicate violet petals and slid the paper across the desk. Mrs Armstrong-Jones nodded.

'Very well,' Linda said. She clicked the mouse and brought up the grid of appointments. 'We could book you in with Angelica at 10am on Thursday if that would be convenient?'

It was. Mrs Armstrong-Jones left, clutching an appointment card and with a much lighter air than she had arrived with. Linda watched her go then returned her attention to the drawing she'd just created.

'I wonder...'

She hesitated for a moment. Should she just speak to Steve? No. In this case, better to bypass him and go straight to the top. Reaching into her handbag, she extracted the mobile she never used. It only had one number stored on it and she pressed the button to dial it.

'Hello Charlie. Yes, it's me. Yes, I know it's been a while. Listen, I need your help. The same kind of help as before. No no, I'm fine. It's not for me this time. It's one of my girls.'

After a few minutes of conversation she ended the call. Extracting the SIM card, she broke it in half. She must remember to get rid of it on the way home and buy a new one.

A few weeks later, Josie phoned in sick. When she eventually came back to work, Linda held her customary 'return from sick leave' meeting.

'Is everything okay, dear?'

Josie bit her lip but nodded.

'I'm alright,' she said. 'It's Mark. He's dead.'

Linda arranged her face into a suitable expression.

'Oh my goodness, what happened?'

'He'd been on a night out with his mates and he fell into the river on his way home. The police said he must have been really drunk.'

A tear ran down her cheek and she dashed it away.

'You poor thing,' Linda said, patting her hand. 'How awful for you. Are you sure you should be here?'

Josie nodded.

'I'm fine, really.' She rubbed a hand over her face. 'I know I should feel sad, but I can't help it. All I feel is relief.' She looked at Linda. 'You knew, didn't you? You knew I was lying about the tin.'

Linda nodded.

'If he'd come home that night, it would have happened again. He just got so angry when he'd been drinking. When he didn't come home, I thought he'd decided to stay at a mate's and I was just so relieved I didn't have to worry about what he'd do. Does that make me an awful person?'

Linda patted her hand again.

'It makes you human.' She tilted her head. 'I know what will make you feel better. How about a little tattoo?'

Josie gave her a watery smile.

'I had been thinking of getting another one,' she said.

Linda passed her a piece of paper. 'A yellow lily, perhaps?'

Josie frowned.

'It symbolises gratitude. You are grateful he's gone, aren't you?'

Josie nodded slowly. 'But how did you...' Her voice trailed off as Linda raised a hand. 'I know. Never ask, just do the task.'

Her employer smiled.

'Good girl. Book yourself in for the tattoo whenever you're ready. It's on the house.'

Josie stood up unsteadily and left the room. Linda sat back in her chair and smiled. Good old Charlie. Family was family after all.

First published in *Makarelle*, 2021 as L.C. Groves

The Merry Maidens

The car engine sputtered and died. I cried aloud in frustration and dashed my hand against the steering wheel, swearing loudly before bursting into equally noisy tears. I'd thought – more hoped – that it would keep going until I was home. Home. A short laugh escaped. I no longer had one of those. I'd left the house I'd lived in for the last ten years and fled across the country, as far from Steven as I could get. Home was now my sister's house in St. Buryan. It wasn't especially small, but with a family of four children, the addition of a wayward sister as a lodger made it feel more than a little crowded at times and I knew I needed to get my own place as soon as I could. That had been the purpose of my trip to Penzance that afternoon, to get some advice from a solicitor friend of my brother-in-law's about where I stood legally. I needed to know if I could force Steven to sell the house, or at least buy out my half of it. His verdict hadn't been particularly encouraging. I could, but it could be a long process if he chose to fight it – which he would – particularly as I had left him. Luckily, Karen had insisted on taking photos of the injuries I'd arrived with and had enlisted the local policeman (another friend of Gary's) to come and take a statement from me at the house.

It had been embarrassing laying out all the details of what I'd been prepared to put up with over the years, all in the name of pride. My parents had been against me marrying Steven in the first place: I was eighteen to his twenty-eight and had no experience of life outside our small town. He already had one divorce behind him and my parents didn't trust him. I didn't care. I was swept up in the thrill of an illicit romance with an older man. We kept our wedding a secret until the register was signed and it had been consummated for fear they would try to stop it.

At first, things were good. My parents gradually accepted my husband and we were happy in our little flat. We decided I didn't need to go to university now I was married and I was happy to get a job and contribute to our life together. Then Steven's job took him to London and he was unhappy commuting, so we moved to the capital.

'I get that you don't want to leave your family Kate, but my job has to come first. It's me that keeps a roof over our heads, remember?'

The last time I went home was for Karen's wedding to Gary. It was a far different affair to our registry office union and I made the mistake of telling Steven that part of me wished we'd done things differently. We had a blazing row. The encounter with Karen over breakfast the next morning was excruciating.

'What have you done to your wrist?'

'Oh, you know what she's like when she's had a drink. Tripped over her dress going up the stairs.'

I nodded quietly, unable to meet my sister's gaze and she narrowed her eyes thoughtfully. She didn't say anything at the time, but she looked at Steven differently after that and it became easier to stay away from family gatherings, especially when she and Gary moved down to Cornwall, although we continued to keep in touch by phone and email.

I couldn't bear to admit my parents had been right and my marriage had been a huge mistake. I began to wonder if he'd told me the truth about why his first marriage had ended. Had his wife really had an affair with his friend, or had she just been a little bit wiser than I was and got out as soon as she was able to? It took me a long time to admit that I needed to get out while I still could and after I'd woken up on a cold kitchen floor for the second time in week to find the house in darkness, I'd thrown whatever clothes I could into a holdall and fled from the house. It hadn't occurred to him to take the car keys with him – I was so cowed by that time I don't think he thought I'd have the courage to leave him. If I'd taken the time to think about what I was doing, he'd probably have been right, but something propelled me out of the door that night before I had the chance to think it through or change my mind.

I phoned Karen from the car and asked her if she could recommend a cheap hotel. I had no money, but I promised to pay her back if she'd just pay for a couple of nights while I found some work.

'Don't be so silly. Come to us and you can stay as long as you need to. You'll be able to find a job to tide you over until you work out what you want to do. I won't hear of you going to a hotel. Let me look after you for a bit.'

Unable to argue I did as I was told and turned up in the early hours of the morning, dishevelled and shaking, to be met with a loving embrace that made me flinch and her weep.

'What has he done to you?'

She had organised me in much the same way as she organised her children – quietly, efficiently and leaving me no room to argue, not that I could have done anyway. The last decade had taught me to be instantly obedient, but Karen never raised her voice if I was too slow to do what she asked. She was gently encouraging and made me take baby steps towards thinking and acting for myself again. The trip to Penzance had been a challenge she'd set me. Could I drive myself there now the adrenaline that had fuelled my initial flight to Cornwall had left me?

'Karen's explained your situation to me,' Tim said when I rang his office, 'So I thought it might be easier for us to talk over a late lunch, make it a bit less formal?'

'That sounds lovely. Thank you.'

We arranged to meet at the Admiral Benbow pub and over a light but surprisingly filling fish pie that melted in your mouth in a creamy froth of butter and cream, followed by the stickiest toffee pudding I'd ever had, he laid out exactly what I could expect to happen over the course of the divorce proceedings. It was daunting to hear it all spelled out and I couldn't help the feeling of failure that crept over me as he talked.

'I've been through this myself,' he said gently, 'And from your face, I suspect you're berating yourself for your marriage not working. From what little Karen shared with me, you did everything you could to make it a success, but sometimes things are just not meant to be and *nobody* should have to put up with what you have.'

My smile was watery, but I made it stick. Karen had told me much the same thing after all. It was going to take some time for me to learn to believe that I hadn't in some way deserved what Steven had done. After all I'd willingly married him behind my parents' back, I'd agreed to move away from my family and had let myself be cut off from everyone except Karen, I'd hurt people who loved me. I wasn't a good person and bad people needed to be punished. But I would do it. I would listen and I would learn.

After we'd eaten, I needed some time to myself, so I'd walked through the streets and around the harbour until it was almost dark and only then did I return to the car. I was so preoccupied that I didn't notice until I was some way out of the town that I had taken a wrong turning somewhere and didn't recognise the road I was on. Pulling into a layby I had a quick look at my phone and was relieved to find my current route only added an extra five minutes to my journey and by a stroke of luck I was still heading in the right direction. As the battery was almost empty, I turned it off, trusting that there would be signs for the village as I got closer.

Typically, the inclement weather which had been threatening all day, arrived as soon as I set off again and the fog rolled in from west so it was like driving through cotton wool. When the warning light flashed up on the car I prayed that whatever was wrong with it wouldn't break down completely until I was safely back at the house, but I'd just driven through Boleigh when the engine coughed and died. I dried my tears and tried to turn my phone on, but it stubbornly refused to show me the Apple logo that would indicate it still had some life in it. I remembered seeing Boleigh on the map and guessed it wasn't too far from my destination, so grabbed my bag and coat from the back seat, locked the car and set off. I couldn't see very much in front of me but reasoned that if I stayed on the main road I would eventually come to the sign for the turning I knew led straight to St. Buryan.

After about half an hour my teeth were chattering, I still hadn't located the turning and I realised with dismay that the ground under my feet was soft and springy. I'd somehow managed to wander off the road and had no idea where I was. Faint sounds drifted through the air but what they were and from which direction they had come I couldn't tell. Night had fallen fully by then and there were no lights for me to head towards in the hope of finding civilisation. It was getting cold though and I knew I had to keep moving if I was going to survive the night. I didn't know the details of how long it took to get hypothermia, but I was pretty sure that sleeping rough on an exposed moor in the middle of November would make me a likely candidate to fall victim to it.

In my confusion, I thought faint echoes of music drifted, the notes carried along on the rolling sea of greyness. Then out of the fog, a figure emerged. I'd never been so glad to see someone in my life. Under one arm he carried what looked like bagpipes.

'I thought I could hear music!'

He smiled. 'Just a small gathering come together in celebration. If you would consent to wait until our gathering is ended, we will see you return safely.'

'Oh that would be wonderful! I broke down on the main road, but my sister's house isn't far from here.'

The fog parted a little as he led me to where the rest of his party were, the sound of the music growing clearer as we drew closer, until flickering torchlight illuminated a small group of dancers accompanied by a lone piper. My rescuer handed me a rough cup filled with a sour tasting drink and wrapped his cloak around my shoulders.

'You look cold,' he said, when I attempted to protest. 'The music and the ale will keep the cold from my bones.'

Then he raised his own pipes to his lips and joined in the merry tune. The ale was stronger than anything I was used to and I felt it thawing me as it slid down my throat. A warm fuzzy feeling spread through my body and I relaxed despite the unusual circumstances in which I found myself, letting the music envelop me and wrap me in a blanket of goodwill. My eyelids drooped in a long blink and the more I forced them open, the quicker they closed again. Even the semi-conscious awareness of strong arms lifting me didn't wake me fully and enjoying the feeling of safety I sank back into the embrace of my dreams.

When my eyes eventually flickered open, bright winter

sunshine assaulted them and I startled, a sharp pain piercing the back of my hand. I looked down at it to see a needle protruding from it.

'Kate?'

Karen's voice trembled, completely at odds with her usual brisk tones.

'How are you feeling?'

'A bit fuzzy. What happened? The last thing I remember is being on the moors. There were people playing music and dancing and the man said if I waited until their party was finished, they'd make sure I got home okay.'

'Kate, your car was found abandoned on the road – it looked like you'd broken down and tried to walk home. The woman who saw the car was concerned, so when she got home she telephoned the police. I'd already rung them to say you were missing, so when the car was registered in your name they called me and we started searching for you. We found you unconscious against one of the Piper stones up by the Merry Maidens and there was no sign of any party up there. You'd obviously taken a blanket out of the car with you, which was sensible, but I don't understand why you didn't stay on the road.'

'It was foggy and I got lost.'

'There was no fog last night. It was as clear as day – the kids were stargazing in the garden.'

I stared at her.

First published on my website, 2019

Archie's Bolero

0:00-0:29

The drumbeat kicks in. Dum de de de Dum de de de Dum de de de Dum. The two figures draped in purple kneel on the ice, their faces almost touching. The music starts and they sway apart, keeping time to the beat. Elegant movements defying the pulse that underpins them. The rat-a-tat-tat of the snare continues to sound.

The man's body is slumped on the sofa. His eyes are trained on the small television set in its wooden cabinet. But his mind is over a thousand miles away. His fingers drum the familiar rhythm on the pink velour upholstery. He tries to bring his mind back from the hillside. He knew they were skating to this tune. Why wasn't he prepared for it? He wasn't prepared then, either.

. . .

Italy, 1944

'Move it!'

The man beside him stumbled, the weight of his equipment propelling him forward. He shot out a hand and steadied him.

'Thanks, mate.'

Archie grinned, his teeth startlingly white against the mud-spattered face.

'Honestly, Drew. I've never known anyone with as much ability to trip over their own feet as you have.'

'Proper talent, innit? Not my fault I've got no co-ordination. We can't all be bleedin' Fred Astaire.'

Archie sighed.

'Astaire's a dancer. I'm a music teacher. Not quite the same thing.'

'Yeah, but it's all music innit. You've gotta have some sense of rhythm to play. Stands to reason it translates to yer feet as well.'

Archie shook his head. They'd had this conversation before. Drew was convinced Archie's musical talents in some way explained his reputation as the best soldier in the platoon. He didn't usually try too hard to persuade him otherwise. It was nice to be admired for a change. When he was younger, his musical abilities had marked him out as different. He was the quiet boy, not interested in football or girls and too often he'd had to fish his music case out of a puddle while other boys laughed at its sodden state.

He and Drew had met at their training camp. They'd shared a lift on the back of a truck going into the village near their base. A dance had been advertised and they'd been given permission to go. They'd arrived and left together, separating only to dance and a friendship had been forged. Archie sensed he'd found a kindred spirit in Drew. It was something about the way he held himself when he danced, as though he was holding a part of himself back.

On their return, they were told that their orders had come in and they were shipping out to the Med at the end of the week.

0:30-1:50

Finally they are on their feet. Their bodies move in perfect synchronisation – two halves of the same person. First one leads, then the other. Always connected. Always supporting. And still the drum beat beneath driving them on.

It had been like that back then as well. Archie and Drew. Inseparable. Even in the valleys below Castle Hill. The rest of the platoon used to joke that they'd been separated at birth. One excelled at spotting the hidden German forces, the other at shooting them. *Except*, he thought, *One of us only pretended to excel. One of us made a mistake.*

Italy, 1944

The slope of the mountain reared above them, the castle at its peak almost invisible from where they crouched.

'How the bleedin' hell are we supposed to get up there?'
'Slowly.'
'Carefully.'
'Can we call a taxi?'

The whispered answers all came at once and the platoon's laughter was quickly smothered. They knew from bitter experience that sound travelled further at night and somewhere above them were German soldiers with machine guns.

"Ere, Archie mate. Didn't you say you 'ad a technique for hillwalking?'

'I hardly think this is the time –'

'Nah mate. Anything you can do to make this easier, you go ahead and share it.'

Archie sighed.

'Do you know Ravel's Bolero?'

'Yeah mate. Course. Me ma used to sing it to us every morning.'

Someone sniggered. Archie ignored it and demonstrated the rhythm of the drum.

'On each heavy beat you put your right foot forward. It takes your mind off the fact you're going uphill.'

'Anything's gotta be worth a try.'

01:51 – 3:15

The woman lies prone across the man's leg – they're obviously at a difficult part of their climb and he takes her face in his hands, reassuring her of his love. He lifts her. She checks they are still heading for the top of the volcano and they continue onwards. She leans on him and he is always there, taking her weight. Supporting her. The volume of the music increases as the dance continues. The drum is more insistent now.

The memories are flooding through him. Insistent. They want to be heard. Richards had been their first casualty that night.

He missed his step and twisted his ankle. Archie and Drew had moved back from their customary position at the head of the platoon to support him. One each side, his arms looped over their shoulders. He told them to leave him. If he recovered, he'd catch them up. If he didn't, he'd see them at the top when the rest of the men caught up. He doesn't want to remember but still his fingers move, stabbing a tattoo into the plush fabric.

Italy, 1944

The looming hulk of the castle was silhouetted against the murderous firework display greeted them as they approached the higher ground.

'Jesus H. Christ.' Webster ducked as another shell exploded somewhere above them.

Archie grinned.

'It's not that bad. You've obviously never experienced a First Form music lesson.' He looked at the teenager's blanched face and touched his arm gently. 'Listen.'

A mortar fired somewhere off to the right of them.

'There's your cymbals.'

A machine gun spat bullets that flew harmlessly over their heads.

'The snare drum.'

An artillery piece boomed to their left.

'There's your bass drum.' He gestured with his rifle. 'And now we add in the high hat.' Webster nodded, his face now determined.

Archie scrambled forward, joining Drew at the head of the men.

'Ready? You spot 'em, I'll down 'em. Just like always.'

3:16 – 4:35

The couple take little running steps, eager now to reach their destination and meet their fate. They cling to each other, faces upturned, reassuring themselves they are doing the right thing. The music is getting steadily louder, the tempo increasing as the end approaches. He lifts her off her feet, twisting her in mid-air, almost flinging her. The mouth of the volcano is in sight. The music rises to a crescendo, the drum beat loud and persistent. Has she reconsidered? Is he angry with her? No. She has complete faith in him. The doggedness of the thudding drum knocks the couple to their knees and together they give themselves over to the mountain. In life they could not be together. In death they cannot be parted.

He knows he doesn't have long left. The doctor made that very clear. She broke the news gently, but she didn't know he welcomed the news. Forty years is a long time to be alone after all. There'd been no-one else. How could there be? He'd been too sad at first. Then there had been the law to consider. By the time it changed it was too late for him. He didn't want to share his life with someone who wasn't *him*. He can feel his heart giving up. He's not surprised – it's been hardened with grief for so long it was bound to wear it down eventually. He can almost feel the arteries folding in on themselves and he smiles as he closes his eyes. *I'm coming*, he thinks. *I won't be long.*

Italy, 1944

All attempts at a silent approach were forgotten as the platoon surged towards the castle. The snare drum accounted for Webster and continued to spit out its unforgiving rhythm until Morris' grenade silenced its steady beat. Bullets ricocheted off the medieval stone. Staccato shots rang out around the hillside. Archie and Drew led their men onwards, taking out enemy troops on all sides.

'Fall back! There's too many of them!'

Wheeling around, the men withdrew back over the hard-won ground, tripping over bodies as they went. They were focused on covering the retreat and no-one saw the arm rise over the low stone wall. An egg-shaped lump of metal landed with a dull thud. Archie and Drew saw it at almost the same time. The muffled explosion was almost anti-climactic: the sound deadened by the body that contained it. The platoon froze in shock. Another of their men was gone. They looked to the other half of the pairing for instructions. He turned and almost without aiming, took out the owner of the arm which had wreaked such devastation. His men urged him to run. He didn't hear them. Eventually, they took his arm and pulled him away with them, leaving half of him behind.

4:36 – 7:42

The couple in purple are back on their feet. They skate over to acknowledge the crowd. Flowers clutched tightly to their chests, their faces are wreathed in smiles and they embrace as the marks are announced. Twelve perfect sixes. Two skaters. Two halves of the same whole in perfect unison.

The pain in his chest is severe, but he barely notices it. He rises from the chair with more ease than he has done in years. *He* is there. *He* has come for him. *He* has waited. They never spoke of it back then. They couldn't. He was never completely sure if his feelings were returned. Now he knows. Now he is complete. The television is replaying the routine and the rhythm sounds again in his head. He smiles.

'On the heavy beat, you put your left foot forward?'

'You never could get the hang of it, could you? It's your

right foot, you twerp.'

His smile becomes a grin. It's time to go.

Background To The Story

In September 1943, following a successful invasion of Sicily, the Allied Armies landed in Italy. The British Eighth Army advanced on north via the Adriatic Coast, whilst the American Fifth Army advanced up the western side of the central mountain range towards Naples. The two armies had three routes to Rome. One was flooded by the Germans, another had an initial breakthrough by the Canadians but had ground to a halt with the onset of winter blizzards. This left Highway 6, through the Liri Valley with Monte Cassino at the southern entrance. The German defences in the area were well fortified and it took four assaults to finally capture Castle Hill. On 17th May 1944, Polish troops captured Monastery Hill and the Battle for Monte Cassino was over.

In 1984 Torvill and Dean won gold at the Winter Olympics in Sarajevo. Their score of twelve perfect 6.0s and six 5.9s made them the highest scoring figure skaters in Ice Dance history. The routine was danced to Ravel's Bolero and the pair have talked about how they came up with a story to inspire them. The story was of two star-crossed lovers who, because they couldn't be together, decided to ascend the volcano and throw themselves to their deaths.

First published in *Makarelle,* 2021

The Few

I stare at the sky; clouds chasing each other, vapour trails cutting a path across the wide blue expanse. The sun is warm on my upturned face but I am cold. I stretch out my suit clad legs, the thick black fabric scratchy and unfamiliar on my skin. I'm more at home in blue chinos these days. They're comfy, you see. Soft. Not like the blue trousers from then. They were rough and didn't fit properly. That's the one thing they never get right in the films – those fighter pilots all look very handsome and terribly British. Most of us didn't have that plummy accent and our uniforms never fit as well as theirs do.

1940 was a scary time for all of us and it feels odd to sit in a cinema and watch it dramatised. No matter how exciting the plot is, the fiction never comes close to capturing the heart-stopping terror we felt. Not that I ever see much of the action. As soon as it starts, I close my eyes and I'm back in the skies, a Messerschmidt 109 on my tail. Every burst of machine gun from the surround sound has me flinching in my seat, certain that every bullet is tracing straight for me. Why do I go, you ask? In some ways the answer is simple and in others it's complicated. The simple answer is: to remember. Every death played out on that screen I saw tenfold. Such films are always dedicated to the memory of 'The Few'. Those few were my friends.

The complicated answer is that I can't help myself. I tell myself not to go. That it doesn't help. It won't bring them back. And yet every time a new one is released, I'm at the front of the queue, urgently thrusting my money at the ambivalent cashier. Sometimes they note my age and comment.

'Reliving old glories, Sir?'

I smile and nod. 'Something like that.' I could never tell them the truth. That there was nothing glorious about it. It was nothing more than a fight for survival. And now I see it all happening again. Different arena. Same lies. Same disaster. It never changes.

I remember because I can't forget. And I wouldn't want to. When we forget, we don't learn the lessons. We make the same mistakes.

There was only me and Fran left from the old days. He never went back after the war. What would have been the point? He was the only one of his family left, so he stayed here with me. We muddled along alright together, him and me. We didn't talk much about the war and he never truly understood my need to see the films, but he was my best friend and now he's gone.

František Svoboda 1921-2022. Beloved and much missed.

It's not much, is it, for a lifetime of companionship? It's more than many of the others got though, so I don't complain. Churchill famously called us The Few and I was proud to be numbered among them. It may have been a living hell at times, but I'd give anything to go back and be with them all.

The Few.
    The Fewer.
    The One.

First published in *Makarelle*, 2022

A Steamy Encounter

I push the door open. A blast of hot air engulfs me as steam billows from the opening. I move inside and cautiously make my way to where I think the benches should be. My boyfriend is in here somewhere but the steam is so thick I can't see him. I grope my way onto a bench and as I lean back my head brushes against a leg. I flinch but a gentle hand reaches down and rests on my shoulder.

'Don't worry.' The voice is muffled.

I frown. It doesn't sound like Neil, but he's so unpredictable I can never tell what kind of games he's going to play. He likes to throw me off my guard.

'I hope I didn't hurt you,' I say. 'I can't see a thing in here.'

'Kind of exciting, isn't it?' the voice says. 'Not knowing who you're sitting with.'

I laugh nervously, not certain how I'm expected to react. I decide to try the playful approach.

'A little. I mean, we could be anyone, couldn't we?'

I hear the amusement in his voice when he speaks again. 'Let's pretend then, shall we? I'm a global megastar escaping from my too-adoring fans for some R and R. Who are you?'

'A bored housewife.' I'm too taken aback to improvise. 'Longing to escape from a partner whose idea of fun is to make me think I'm losing the plot. This is a rare escape from him and the house.' I wince as the words tumble out, wondering if Neil will recognise the truth behind the words.

To my surprise, he says nothing, but slides down from the upper seat and sits next to me, his arm snaking around my shoulder. It rests there for a moment before he speaks again.

'So I'm hounded and you have a terrible partner. We meet and then what?'

'You ride to my rescue and we live happily ever after?' I'm still not sure what he wants me to say, but I figure this will appeal to his need to see himself as the hero of the story.

His hand strays a little further but I stay relaxed, curious now. What does he have in mind? His behaviour is very un-Neil like. It's gentle and undemanding. The hand slides beneath my bikini top and I gasp.

'Don't worry, no-one will see,' he murmurs. 'I can't even see you!'

My response is a strangled moan. My back arches as pleasure surges through me and I turn my face to his. His lips find mine and for a moment I forget where we are. When we eventually break apart he kisses the sensitive skin below my ear.

'I have a room booked, would you like take this upstairs?' His voice is suddenly hesitant, the customary self-assurance missing.

I had no idea he'd booked us in overnight, but the idea is suddenly appealing. In these last minutes I've seen a side of him I didn't know existed and it's incredibly sexy.

'Meet in Reception?' I manage, between kisses.

'Mmhh.'

I slide out from between his arms and check nothing is exposed, then leave the steam room. As I hurry towards the changing rooms, Neil emerges from the men's toilets. I look at him in shock.

'Where the fuck are you going?' he demands.

'The toilet,' I improvise. 'It's too hot in there for me. You go in though.'

'You're always like this. Can't take the heat, can you? Pathetic.' He sneers and walks away.

In the changing room, I towel myself dry and throw my clothes on in record time. I feel free for the first time in months. In the mirror, the face that stares back at me is flushed with sparkling eyes. It's an expression I've lost sight of but I welcome its return.

I make my way into the foyer, pausing for a moment to glance at a poster advertising an upcoming gig by the latest big-name singer. The name means nothing but the date is today's. He has his back to me when I see him, but instantly I know it's him. The wet hair is an instant give-away, but it's more than that; a gut feeling. He turns and his eyes light up when he sees me a few steps away. I feel a jolt of recognition. I know his face. He extends a hand to me and his mouth crinkles into a boyish grin. I return the smile, my mind racing. Have we met before?

As we cross to the lift, I see another poster like the one in the corridor. My eyes slide from the image of the singer to the man holding my hand and I suppress a gasp. It seems I'm not the only one who lacks imagination.

Wyndham's Oak

11 June 2015, Wyndham's Oak, Dorset

Emily leant back against the broad trunk of the tree, closed her eyes and breathed in deeply. Her father was always a proponent of the benefits of fresh air and she certainly needed them. She was waiting for Iain and he was late as usual. *He'll be with her again, no doubt. She'll have made an excuse to delay him.* There was always an excuse. Emily had known his reputation before they got together but she convinced herself she could change him. She would be different. She'd be the one to keep him. Instead, she spent their time apart wondering what *they* were doing. Whether he professed his love for her. Whether he was going to leave. Emily had made a decision though and told him they needed to talk. She was tired of being messed about.

Something brushed against her forehead and she swatted it away impatiently. *It would be just my luck to get a mosquito bite in the middle of my face today of all days. I've got to tell him that it's time to make his mind up. Her or me.* That's why she'd asked him to meet her by the tree. She'd been teaching her class about the Monmouth rebellion earlier that week and it had inspired her to be bold. They'd hung some of Monmouth's supporters on the very spot she was now sitting on, when the rebellion failed and she admired that they were willing to fight (and die in some cases) for what they wanted. For what they believed they were owed. She wanted to make a point. She and Iain had been together for two years now. She'd waited long enough.

Something brushed her face again. She opened her mouth as she swatted it away again. Then screamed. A pair of feet dangled in front of her face, the lace from the white socks encasing the legs must have been what had tickled her. Backing away in horror, she felt the rough bark of the trunk scratch her back through the thin sundress as she slid up the tree, unable to bear the thought of that *thing* touching her again. She moaned quietly as she realised her bag was still on the floor. Backing around the side of the tree, she stretched an arm out and groped blindly for the strap, pulling it towards her in relief as her fingers closed around the thin leather. Stumbling slightly, her feet catching on the uncut grass, she hurled herself away from the tree, the breath catching in her throat. Iain would have to think what he wanted when she wasn't there to meet him. She couldn't stay there, not in that place. Not with the ghost.

High in the branches of the tree, concealed by the broad swathe of foliage, Melissa stifled a giggle. *It was almost too easy*, she thought, as she hauled the dummy back into the tree. Iain had never been the most subtle of people and she'd found out about his wandering eye not long after their marriage. She stayed with him because of the children mainly, but this time he'd seemed different. She wasn't going to beg him to stay – quite the reverse actually, she'd packed his bags ready for when he got home later – but she was damned if she was going to let them get off scot-free. Putting the fear of God into Emily had been fun but it was almost too easy. For a teacher of history she was amazingly gullible and loved to see ghosts everywhere. (Melissa had discovered that little pearl of information via Iain's credit card statement – the ghost hunting trip certainly hadn't been purchased for her.) Melissa smiled grimly. *Oh yes*, she thought. *I've got far more fun planned for those two.*

First published on Dorset Tree Festival website, 2021

Cake

Emily glared at her husband. 'Why do you always do this? It's every time we go out!'

'I don't know what you're talking about.'

'You know exactly what I'm talking about. Every time we go anywhere you provoke an argument.'

'No I don't. All I said was that I thought the Egyptian stuff was boring and why couldn't we look at something else. That's not provoking an argument.'

'It is when you know that we came here specifically because I wanted to see the Egyptian stuff.'

'Sshh.'

'Don't tell me to shush.'

'Well don't shout then. You're so bloody Northern. Why does everything have to be at full volume?'

'It isn't,' Emily hissed. 'And even if it was, it just shows how angry you make me. Why can't you be supportive of my interests?'

'I am supportive. We're here aren't we? Being supportive doesn't necessarily mean loving everything as much as you do. And you're still shouting. People are looking.'

'Do I look like I care? If people are so interested in our business let them listen. Nosy buggers.'

She glared at a rather startled looking old lady, who suddenly found a nearby statue completely fascinating.

'Some people are so rude!' Emily tossed her head disdainfully and moved further into the room away from the offending woman.

'This one's nice, isn't it?'

'Don't start pretending to take an interest. You've already made your feelings quite clear, thank you!'

'I'm not pretending. I do like this one.'

'Oh whatever. You go if you want to. I'll just look round on my own.'

'Don't be like that. Come on.' David pulled his wife's arm through his own. 'Show me what you wanted to see.' He flashed her a grin. 'If you're a good girl I'll take you to the café after and buy you cake.'

Emily suppressed a grin. 'Don't think you can get round me with offers of cake.'

'What about if I throw in a cup of tea as well?'

'Make it coffee and I'll think about forgiving you.'

'Deal.'

Arms linked, they headed towards the case containing the Rosetta Stone.

The Garden Of Eden

Derek rested his head against the back of the coach seat and allowed his wife's shrill complaints to wash over him. He was in no danger as long as he nodded his head occasionally and murmured noises of agreement.

'Derek, are you even listening to me?'

'Of course, dear. You're absolutely right.'

Eyes narrowed, but apparently satisfied, Margaret subsided back into her own seat and resumed her monologue. Not listening to the detail, but conscious he had almost been caught out, Derek gathered she was unhappy about the lack of superior seating the coach company had promised and believed it would have been better if they had driven to The Eden Project after all. He forbore to point out that the coach had been her idea – in fact she had insisted on it – as Derek's driving made her feel sick. *If my driving is so awful, why do I have to do all of it? She could have driven to the other end of the bloody country.*

'Really Derek, I do think you could have checked that the seating arrangements were as advertised before booking the trip.'

Does she ever stop blethering on? My God, woman. Just shut up.

'I'm terribly sorry, dear. You're absolutely right of course.'

Margaret huffed and snatched up her paperback, returning to *A Cornish Escape*.

'Is your book good?' Derek ventured, knowing he was expected to ask.

'Not bad. Woman's got a backbone at least.'

He knew that was his wife's pet hate in fiction. Weak women horrified her. In her view, women were the superior gender and they'd been suppressed for too long. The only person allowed to made decisions for Margaret Rufford was Margaret herself. Derek's only role was to work and support her choices for their life together. He'd long since given up trying to argue with her – he got more response from the dog than from his wife – and retreated into the safety of his own mind and his garden. There at least he was allowed an opinion.

He missed his shed. It was quiet in there and he liked the smell of wet earth and tomatorite. Cornwall was pretty but unlike in Margaret's book, it was no escape for him. He opened his own book *Death in the Garden: Poisonous Plants and Their Use Throughout History*.

'I don't know how you can read such morbid nonsense,' Margaret tutted.

I can dream, can't I?

'It's just a book,' he said mildly. 'It's interesting, that's all. You know I like my garden.'

'Of course I know. That's why we're doing this ridiculous trip in the first place! Heaven knows, I have no interest in plants!'

Eventually, the coach pulled into the carpark and disgorged its passengers, who milled around, waiting for their representative to sort out their entrance tickets.

'Come along, Derek. It's taken us long enough to get here. If we don't hurry, we won't have time to see everything.'

She shouldered her way through the small groups clustered together, ignorant of the hissed comments and black looks that followed her. Derek followed in her wake, quietly apologising as his wife moved out of earshot.

When the couple didn't return to the coach at the end of the day, nobody said anything, but there was a collective sigh of relief as the coach pulled out of the car park to begin the journey back to St. Ives. It was only those who read the small article tucked away on page four of the next day's local paper who even gave them a second thought.

HOLIDAYMAKER IN EDEN DEATH PLUNGE

A 52 year old woman has died after falling from one of the high walkways at local tourist spot, The Eden Project. Her husband who was the only witness to the appalling tragedy apparently told onlookers that his wife had been leaning over the side to take a photograph and had dropped her camera. As she lunged to catch it, she lost her balance and went over the railings. Cornwall police were unavailable for comment at the time of printing.

First published on my website, 2019

The Injured Queen Of England

The heat shimmers in the air above the gardens. Sweat slides between my breasts, under my stays and pools beneath my arms. My body is slick with it and yet I am cold. Frozen. God has judged me and I have been found wanting. Charlotte is dead. The one truly good thing in my life is gone and I cannot even say goodbye to her. He will not allow it. My gaze falls on the barren branches of the dead tree at the bottom of the villa's garden and I cannot help but compare myself to it. I too have been stripped bare, denuded of all dignity, denied even a covering of de- cency.

I never should have married him. What kind of man doesn't even have the courtesy to tell his wife when their only daughter dies in childbirth? I'll tell you what kind – the kind who sends his mistress to meet his fiancée when she first arrives in his country. Even the people of England saw the offence in that. Prince of Whales they call him now. How he must hate it – such a cruel moniker for someone so vain about his appearance. I wonder which he hates most – that name or me?

Hate has always burned strong between us. They say it's the closest emotion to love, but I disagree. I cannot bring myself to be indifferent to the man who has humiliated me at every turn. But even for him this is low. I had to find out about the death of my daughter and grandson from a sympathetic courier on his way to the Pope.

The Whale has tried everything to destroy me and yet here I sit. I have a man who loves me, a comfortable home and the support of the common people of England, but without my darling girl, it means nothing. She stood by me when he turned his back. There were others who did so, but I know deep down that many of those who encouraged me did so because they hated him not because they loved me. She was a symbol of hope to so many – their future Queen when the mad one and the fat one are dead. But she was more than a princess to me. She was my support, my reason to live.

I miss her laughter. I miss her love.

I miss her.

In the years that have passed since my dear Charlotte's death, I have grown reckless. I no longer care what people think of me, or at least that's what I tell myself. When you've been accused of bedding half your household and of bearing multiple illegitimate children, you grow accustomed to the sideways glances and the knowing looks. The advantage of age is that you no longer have to take heed of them.

When I left England I had choices again. I could have returned to Brunswick, but that would have been a step back. I wanted to get away from my marriage and my husband, yes, but not to return meekly to my father's house. Alone. In disgrace. No thank you. I wanted to live. To have the life I should have had. The life I deserved. So, I came here to Italy.

The other advantage of age is that you be- come more aware of your own value. My father may have admitted I was ignorant (and if I am, whose fault is that?), but whilst my education was lacking, I know the importance of public opinion and I've learned how to use it to my advantage. A regent who spends all his country's money on his own wardrobe and flaunts his mistresses, whilst complaining that his wife does the same, was never going to be popular. Meanwhile, his poor put-upon wife, cast out of polite society and threatened at every turn? She is a figure of sympathy. Of pity. And if she misbehaves in her turn, well who can blame her? A woman is weak, in need of protection. If her feeble mind and body turn to a man for support when her husband has abandoned her for another, is it truly her fault? Not if you know how to sway public opinion. A word or two in the right ear is all it takes.

Now the Whale is king, he thinks to seek a divorce. James Brougham may believe he has all the evidence he needs of my adultery, but the Whale will only get his divorce if I get my money. He thought he was so clever putting spies in my household, but Barty was one step ahead of them and we made sure there was no evidence to find. A few months of public propriety did us no harm. Thank the heavens there are some very secluded parts of the grounds or I should have been driven mad. Lady Jersey and Mrs Fitzherbert are welcome to my husband. I know what it is like to be made love to and whatever happened on my wedding night, it was not lovemaking, for all that it resulted in Charlotte. It may not be fashionable or 'proper' for a lady to seek pleasure or for a man to be concerned with giving it, but I have never understood why such separation exists. When Barty visits his wife, I ache for him. When he returns it is all I can do not to beg him to make love to me right there in the hallway. How shocked the servants would be!

A cold fish like Brougham could never understand that. All he thinks about are titles and money. I would have been less insulted if he had called me a strumpet than by what he offered. Duchess of Cornwall, indeed! I became the Princess of Wales on my marriage and that I will remain. The Whale calls his father a mad old goat, but it's he who is mad if he thinks I'll accept anything less than my due.

The Whale won't pay. The only way to be rid of him is to admit adultery and it is impossible for me to do that. Not because it's untrue – I can deny Barty nothing – but because to do so would be to play into the Whale's hands. If I admit to being unfaithful, I lose everything. I don't care about my name or reputation – Charlotte often told me to be happy – but I need money to live on. Barty has financial needs as well as physical ones and he must be kept happy. He has a family to support and without me he has nothing. He gave up everything to be with me and I can- not let him down. We are headed for France soon. Even half a decade on it feels strange to say that. For so long the little man made travelling on the Continent a perilous undertaking. Perhaps Louis could be persuaded to give me an audience? The Whale admired him greatly when he was in England. Would his support make my husband see reason? Perhaps I should threaten to return to England. I still have the support of the people and the Whale knows how easily I can encourage unrest amongst them. That threat alone should make the Whale realise I cannot and will not be dismissed so easily.

My decision is made. I am for England. The Whale is King and legally I am still his wife. I am Queen. I have no desire to live with him though. I want only to return to Italy and Barty. My body longs for his touch – it has been too long and I crave the scent of him on mys kin –but I have a job to do first. The Whale seems set on making my life as difficult as possible. To be addressed as the Duchess of Brunswick! I have no doubt that particular insult was of his making, even if it was delivered by Cardinal Consalvi. Odious little man.

If the Whale will not let me go, he must accept my presence. It may not be 'His Majesty's pleasure to comply' with my application to attend the coronation, but His Majesty is going to discover I have no care for his pleasure. Perhaps if I make enough of a scene, he will give me my divorce and I will be free to return to my love. Barty is using my absence to return to Her, but he must come back to the villa as soon as I return. His last letter assured me of his continued devotion and his words – though doing nothing to ease my longing for him – promise he is still as much mine as he ever was.

Victory is mine! I have my £50,000 and no conditions. They tried everything to deprive me of it, but I had the last laugh. And the loudest. 'I did commit adultery once – with the husband of Mrs Fitzherbert.' I'm not sure which was the bigger joke, my words or my marriage. He was never mine. I'm not sure he was ever truly anyone's, but at least he belonged to Mrs Fitzherbert and Lady Jersey for a while. How ironic that he married to pay off his debts and I had to threaten divorce to pay off mine. At least now I am free to do as I please.

I think I will still attend the Coronation though. He cannot stop me after all. It is my right as Queen. One last humiliation for him before I leave. A parting gift from his wife, to ensure the occasion is a memorable one. A final public outing and then I can return to Barty. I can almost feel the Italian sun warming my skin. It pours through the window of our bedroom and I love watching it illuminate his bare skin, as his fingers dance across my flesh. My skin tingles at the thought. Not long now.

. . .

We arrive at Westminster Hall early and Lord Hood escorts me to the door. My chamberlain is loyal to a fault and he was determined to accompany me. I am under no illusion that I will be granted access, but if it is not to be, then I will make it as uncomfortable a day as possible for the Whale. He has waited so long to be king in name as well as deed and I cannot let him enjoy his triumph. The crowd are pleased to see me, as I knew they would be. The soldiers guarding the door are less so. They close the door and demand to see my ticket. I feign indignance and draw on my years of training. Shoulders back. Head up. Intimidating glare.

'I am the Queen. I have no need of a ticket.'

They refuse to move, as I knew they would. We try another entrance and meet with a similar reception. Lord Hood suggests a third door, but the path to it is guarded by a line of armed soldiers. We are also denied entry at the House of Lords. The Whale really does not want me at his coronation. I suppress a smile.

'Never mind, Lord Hood, we will go straight to the abbey instead.'

When we arrive, dear Hood suggests I wait in the carriage until he speaks to the rather ferocious looking doorkeeper – there are rumours the Whale has hired professional boxers, such is his unpopularity. I refuse to be cowed by them. I alight from the carriage and Hood hurries ahead of me.

'I present to you your queen, do you refuse her admission?'

'I'm sorry, Lord Hood. I have strict instructions to admit no one without a ticket, regardless of their rank.'

The poor man is puce with embarrassment. Beneath the rounded vowels full of effort, I hear the coarsened tones of the East End. He must be one of the boxers the Whale has hired to keep me out. I feel a slight twinge of guilt. It's not his fault. He needs the job.

'I have a ticket, man! The queen is with me.'

'I'm sorry,' the hapless man repeats. 'Your ticket is only for one person. I can't admit two of you.' He wrings his hands, then his face brightens and I realise he's on my side. I'm not sure how this makes me feel. 'Perhaps you could give Her Majesty your ticket?' He looks like a hopeful puppy.

To my horror, Lord Hood nods thoughtfully. He turns to me.

'Your Majesty?'

I shake my head. 'Attend unaccompanied? Impossible! I am the Queen of England!'

Lord Hood turns back to the man and entreats him to allow us entry. Again, he is refused. I am glad. I have no wish to go inside. My life with the Whale was over long ago, thank the heavens. I only wished to show him what he could have had if he had given our marriage a chance. The people love me and with me at his side, they could have loved him. He didn't even give it a chance. There is a small part of me that still wonders what might have been, but it is buried beneath years of scorn and humiliation. I thought revenge would be more satisfying, but I feel nothing beyond the desire to leave this country and all its memories behind me.

As we drive away, listening to the chants of 'shame, shame' from the waiting crowds, Lord Hood's head droops.

'I am sorry, your Majesty,' he murmurs. 'I failed you.'

I lean over and pat his hand.

'Not in the least,' I assure him. 'It went splendidly.'

I sit back and rest my head against the plush seat. A sharp pain lances across my stomach and I close my eyes. I will be back with Barty soon. Some milk of magnesia to settle my stomach this evening and I will begin making arrangements to return to Italy.

. . .

Caroline of Brunswick died three weeks later. Her husband, George IV survived her by nine years. Her will stated that she wished to be buried in Brunswick and her coffin was to bear the inscription 'Here lies Caroline, the injured Queen of England'. George IV's ministers were worried her funeral procession would cause public unrest and so a route was planned which avoided the city of London. The people of London had other ideas however, and blocked the planned route to force the procession through the city.

On her way to Harwich, Caroline's coffin rested overnight in St. Peter's Church, Colchester and it was here that her executors tried unsuccessfully to replace the official inscription plate with one bearing the phrase Caroline had requested.

First published in *Makarelle*, 2022

The Edinburgh Tattoo

'Come on Gran.' Min shouted from the steps above her and Angela staggered to join her, feeling every one of her seventy-one years. The beat of the drums far below was just beginning and she still had several rows to climb. The musicians in their best military uniforms were ready to begin and she pushed on, wanting to be in her seat before they took to the parade ground. She flopped down heavily onto the plastic seat and took a moment to appreciate the backdrop of the castle, lit up by coloured floodlights. She felt the usual current of excitement tingling in her nerve endings as she heard the distinctive wail of the inflating bagpipes

'I don't know why you put yourself through this every year, Mum.' Martha had already settled in her seat and stowed her coat underneath it. Now, her arms were folded and her face drawn into a frown. 'Would you even recognise him now? And if you did, would you want to?'

How could her daughter ask? She'd recognise him anywhere. She knew she would. His hair probably didn't curl just over his collar anymore and the brown was likely to be shot through with silver, or perhaps it was gone completely. The smooth cheeks would be more crumpled than they had been, but his smile wouldn't have changed. His smile had dazzled her, blinding her to everything but the need to be with him. In 1967 she'd just completed her final year at Edinburgh university but had returned for a farewell trip to the Tattoo. Her first visit had been just before the start of her university life and it had become a tradition that she went to the last night of the festival. Even in the difficult years that followed, she'd always made it and it had become a kind of pilgrimage. When her daughter was old enough she'd been included in the trip and in later years, her granddaughter also went with them. Angela suddenly realised Martha was still talking.

'Why would you want to see him again anyway? We've always been alright, haven't we?'

Angela reached over and squeezed her daughter's hand. Dear Martha. Always so prickly. How could she possibly understand though? She'd only been with David a few months but Angela could tell her daughter was already getting bored. Martha never let anyone close to her for too long. Men were necessary for the procuring of a child and once she had Min she saw no need for further long term entanglements.

Martha's experience of being a single parent were vastly different to Angela's. By the time Min was born, single mums were no longer the social pariahs they'd been thirty years earlier. Martha had no need of the old brass curtain ring that still sat in Angela's jewellery box, nestled between earrings of semi-precious stones and silver bracelets. She hadn't worn it for years – eventually she'd saved enough to buy a cheap wedding ring and called herself a widow – but she kept it as a reminder of how hard she'd had to work to eke out a decent life for the two of them. Martha thought her mother was morbid to keep looking backwards, but how could she explain that she had no choice in the matter? Martha was such a different personality, constantly looking for the next new thing. How could someone like that possibly comprehend the tie that kept her bound even after all these years?

She'd known from the start there was no future in it, but she'd allowed herself to be carried along on the wave of love – there was a good proportion of lust mixed in there as well if she was honest – and not given much thought to the time beyond those magical few days.

'I hate the bloody bagpipes.' She'd laughed at the overheard comment and turned to see the man next to her scowling at the pipers far below them.

'Why on earth are you here then?' The words had escaped before she'd had time to think them through, but he grinned lopsidedly at her.

'I don't like wasting money,' he said. 'My wife was meant to come with me, but she changed her mind at the last minute and insisted I came without her. She's the one who likes all this stuff.'

Angela smiled sympathetically. She loved the pomp and circumstance of it all, but even she had to admit the bagpipes weren't her favourite part of the show.

'Marie can be... difficult,' he said, his mouth twisting with the words. 'That makes her sound awful, I know and I don't mean it to. It's just, complicated, I suppose. I'm Michael, by the way.'

Angela took his hand and shook it, introducing herself. They quickly settled into an easy conversation and talked all night, walking through the darkened streets of the capital long after the Tattoo had finished. Neither of them wanted to break the fragile threads that spun around them by parting and they saw sunrise from Arthur's Seat high above the city. The air felt fresh and clean and full of the promise of a beautiful late summer day. When he kissed her, just as the sun appeared above the horizon, she knew she was in love. She didn't believe in love at first sight. It was a ridiculous notion. But the truth of it was, there was no other way to describe how she felt. They walked back to her hotel, oblivious to the sounds and smells of the city as it came back to life. The last night of the festival was the culmination of weeks of events and there was an air of resignation in the flapping of abandoned leaflets and torn posters advertising the various Fringe acts. Edinburgh's time to shine had passed for another year.

She began missing him the moment he let go of her hand. A few hours later, he picked her up again and they had lunch in a tiny café tucked away behind Grassmarket. People chatted around them, but it was just noise. In their bubble there was only silence and they drank each other in along with the dry white. He held her hand while they ate and it was inevitable that their post lunch walk took them back to his hotel. They'd spent the next two days in bed, ordering room service to avoid separating for any length of time.

When the time came for her to leave he wiped her tears away and hid his own.

'I wish things could be different,' he said. 'I can't bear it.'

She told him she wished the same, but they both knew how things stood between them. Michael couldn't abandon his marriage – he owed Marie more than that – and Angela had no wish to become embroiled with a married man. Better for them both to pretend it was nothing more than a fling and return to their separate lives.

Martha had been born in 1968.

Angela's parents had been appalled and she'd moved back to Edinburgh. Away from their anger and their shame. Away from everyone who knew her. She found work and a sympathetic landlady in the same bed and breakfast and saved until she could afford proper childcare and a flat of her own. That was when she began calling herself Mrs Townsend and started working at the solicitor's office in the typing pool. Eventually she worked her way up the ladder and became secretary to the senior partner in the firm with responsibility for overseeing the girls in the room she'd begun in.

'Nan? Are you okay?'

Min's voice cut through her thoughts and she turned to smile reassuringly at her. Angela hadn't been sure about the name 'Araminta' when Martha had chosen it, but she liked it well enough now. It seemed to suit the wayward curls and slender form. Min was a talented artist and was off to art college in a few weeks. She had every ounce of her mother's drive and determination but there was a softer side to her as well and this came out in the beautiful things she created.

'I'm fine, darling. Just reminiscing.'

Angela's eyes scanned the faces of the people nearest to her. After all these years it was unlikely she would see him, but she clung to the hope that one day he might return. She'd often thought of Michael over the years. Wondering if he was happy; feeling sad and guilty that he'd never got to know his daughter and granddaughter. Coming back to the Tattoo was a ritual now. She'd long given up hope of seeing him there. Or at least, that's what she told Martha. A small part of her still clung to the idea of running into him again. It was a million to one chance, she was sensible enough to recognise that, but nothing could kill that tiny flame of optimism.

As the first triumphant march ended and the final notes died away, there was a tap on her shoulder and she turned. A man with thick grey hair stood in the aisle at the side of her. He gave her a lopsided grin.

'I still hate those bloody bagpipes.'

Angela stared at him for a moment, then rose unsteadily to her feet, a smile tugging at the corners of her mouth.

'Why are you here then?'

'Looking for a girl I once knew.'

Angela held her hand out to him. 'Well I'd hate for you to have wasted your money. Maybe we could look for her together.'

First published in *Makarelle*, 2021

Coming Home To Cornwall

My foot inches closer to the floor as my car devours the miles of the A30. Ahead of me, just coming into view I can see them. One hundred and forty beech trees grouped together in a little copse at the top of a hill. 'Welcome home,' they say. Will I be welcome though? Have I become an emmet in my absence? When I left, approaching them from the opposite direction, I noticed a single tree further down the hill. It looked as though the others had all turned their backs on it because it had left their group to explore new pastures. I was excited for it then. It was off to new adventures. Now I just felt sorry for it.

I thought my life was beginning when I left Cornwall, but five years later, here I am, driving down the same old road, returning to the county of my birth. It's an old story, told for ever more in romantic comedies: girl meets boy, girl and boy fall in love, girl follows boy back to the big city, girl and boy marry. Boy dies. Yeah, maybe that last bit isn't quite as funny. I could have stayed there, I suppose, I had a job, friends, a life. None of it meant anything though. Not without him. And so I decided to move back home. Not to my parents' house – I couldn't do that again. But back to Cornwall at least. Somewhere I can heal.

I risk another glance at the trees and I feel something settle over me. A sense of calm I haven't felt since Tim died. There's something so reassuringly solid about them. They've been there all my life, welcoming us home whenever we went on holiday. Someone would always say, 'Almost home now,' whenever we saw them. We weren't of course – there was still almost an hour of driving left, but we were on the final stretch at least.

The trees are famous in their own right now. Nobody truly knows why they were planted there, but they've been welcoming people to Cornwall for over a hundred years. They've been immortalised in paintings and prints and sold by the thousand all across the county under different titles. Trees are said to have great healing qualities and to some extent it's true – I've walked miles through woodlands in the last few months. These ones are different though. They're more than just trees. For me they're simply, home.

First published on the Dorset Tree Festival website, 2021

It's a funny thing, death. Happens to everyone. No one wants to talk about it. You know it will come looking for you eventually, but you don't expect it to find you at twenty-one.

In Memoriam

Michael Joseph Townsend

25.1.1998 – 31.7.2019

Michael's parents wanted to allow friends and family to share some of their memories of Michael, who was taken from us far too early. His star will continue to shine.

I thought when I married my wife, Lisa, that would be the happiest day of my life, but it was soon eclipsed by the day Michael was born. Becoming a father was and still is, the proudest moment of my life. As anyone who knows me will testify, I'm not one for big emotional displays. I don't find it easy to say how I feel. Michael understood that I think and I have to trust that in spite of that, he knew how much I loved him. I didn't tell him very often, but Michael and I got each other, we really did.

I used to take him to the rugby when he was younger. He'd take a little suitcase with him that had colouring books and pencils in for when he inevitably got bored. Lisa would pack some sweets for him as well and by half-time, he'd have made friends with all the fans around him and be sharing his sweets with them. He retained that ability to make friends right through to adulthood. Everyone loved Michael and I often envied him his ability to just walk into a room of strangers and start talking to them. He seemed to instinctively know what made people tick and how to engage them. He wasn't selfish though – if you were with him, he'd drag you along in his wake and include you in the conversation as well, as I'm sure Neil will testify. When they were teenagers, I got home from work one day and found them in the living room, heads together and thought they were getting on with some homework project. But when I went to look at what they were doing, Michael was suggesting various strategies they could use to attract the girls in their year. His approach was methodical, scientific and evidence-based. I wasn't sure whether to be horrified or impressed at his rigour!

When Fliss came along though, I knew she was the one for Michael and I think he knew it too. Lisa and I hoped they'd stay together and we'd have some grandchildren, but it wasn't to be. Life has a nasty habit of getting in the way of the best laid plans and it decided to take Michael away from us all. I hope that wherever he is, he's at peace, while those of us who have been left behind do our best to continue life without him.

Joe Townsend

Writing a eulogy for their child is something no parent ever envisages having to do. Michael was my baby. I was only eighteen when he was born, not much more than a child myself and I was terrified of getting it wrong. But he was such an easy baby and as he grew up, he turned into a son to be proud of. He was loyal and loving and there was nothing he wouldn't do for his family and friends.

Right from being small, Michael was always the centre of attention and one of my favourite memories is of watching him singing and dancing in our living room when he was about five years old. He was out of tune and had no sense of rhythm, but he didn't care.

He continued to show that level of enthusiasm into his adult life, when he left school and joined Entwhistle Grey. He loved being an estate agent and helping to match people with their dream homes. I know he was looking forward to starting the search for his own first home with Fliss and I'm so grateful to him for bringing her into our lives. I hope she knows how happy she made him.

Michael was loved by so many and I know how much he'll be missed by all who knew him, but as his mother, there are no words to express how big a hole he leaves in my life. Nothing can ever fill that missing part of me. Rest in peace, darling boy.

Lisa Townsend

> He that is thy friend indeed,
>> He will help thee in thy need:
>> If thou sorrow, he will weep;
>> If thou wake he cannot sleep;
>> Thus of every grief in heart
>> He with thee doth bear a part.
>> There are certain signs to know
>> Faithful friend from flattering foe.

How do you write a eulogy for your best mate? Mike and I have been friends since we were eleven years old. A whole decade of friendship to try to summarise into a handful of words. Richard Barnfield's poem sums up what friendship is and whenever I read it, I always think of Mike.

We met on our first day at County High and we hit it off straight away. We weren't the most obvious choice of friend for each other – he was loud, confident and sporty, I was quiet, shy and a bit of a geek. But for whatever reason, he decided we were going to be friends and once Mike decided you were on his team, that was it, you were in. Being friends with him meant I didn't get bullied at secondary school and I'll be forever grateful for that. I was the kind of kid who was an easy target and being friends with Mike meant I didn't have to worry about that.

Growing up, we were always getting into scrapes together and I remember one time daring each other to do ever more elaborate tricks at the skate park. Of course, I was the one who came off and broke my arm, but it was Mike who called my Mum, Mike who brought the get well cards and homework from school and Mike who was first to sign my cast. He was almost the only one to sign it because he wrote his name so big there was barely any room for anyone else! That was typical Mike. He wasn't afraid to tell you how he felt and it was one of the things I most admired about him. He was so confident he didn't care what anyone else thought. If he wanted something, he'd just go out and get it.

Mike always included me in everything, even after we left school. I was with him the night he met Fliss and I thought once they got serious I'd see less of him, but whenever I was home from university, he'd still insist I went out with them, made me part of a group with him and Fliss. When I came home after graduation, he started making plans for all the things we were going to do and I still can't quite believe he's gone. Of all of us, Mike was the one who was most full of life. He never let an opportunity pass him by and I owe it to him to live the rest of my life the way he would have done: I'll be living for both of us. Rest in peace mate.

Neil Fletcher

The first time I met Mike, he quite literally swept me off my feet. I'd never met anyone like him before: so determined and so sure of what he wanted. He mentioned marriage right from the start and although I knew it was only a chat-up line, he soon made it clear it was where we were heading eventually.

With Mike, I felt there was always someone on my side, that I was protected. Mike had enough confidence for both of us and whenever my courage failed, he lent me some of his. Put simply, he was the best boyfriend I could ever have hoped for.

We met by chance on a night out in Chelmsford and I fell for him the moment I saw him. I couldn't believe my luck when he said he felt the same. He could have chosen anyone, but he wanted me. I felt lucky that night and he continued to make me feel that way throughout our relationship.

I was nervous about him meeting my mum, but he charmed her, just as he charmed everyone he met. He came to a work's night out with me once and spent the whole evening chatting to my boss. The next day I was given a pay rise. I never found out what he'd said, but my boss assured me it was all down to Mike. That was Mike all over – he could get anyone to do anything he wanted them to. He even taught me see my own value.

I was so blessed to spend a year with Mike and if that's all the time we were allowed, then I have to be grateful for that. So many people never get to experience love and I had the best year with him.

For someone who works with words on a daily basis, I'm struggling to find the ones that will adequately convey the sense of loss I feel. Mike was more than just my boyfriend; he was my soulmate and with his death I've lost a part of myself. Good night my darling and sleep safely.

Felicity Stanmore

They say when you die, your life flashes before your eyes. It don't. There's just pain. So much pain. Regrets though? Not me. Never regretted a thing.

JOE

I can't do this anymore. I've told so many lies about Michael over the last few months. I loved…love (because his death hasn't altered this fact) my son dearly, but I can't keep pretending he was some kind of saint. Lisa talks about him as though he never did anything wrong and I suppose from her perspective he didn't. I never told her. I can't tell her now. We don't really talk anymore, haven't done for months. I'm failing her, just as I failed him. Maybe if I'd confronted him with what I knew, talked to him about his behaviour, he wouldn't have even been in the car that morning.

I slam my hand on the desk, angry at it for shaking, for betraying my weakness. I have to get my life back under control somehow. Alan was right about that.

'You're a good man, Joe and you've worked for me for a long time. I'm talking to you as a friend, not just your boss. If you don't get the drinking under control, I'll have to let you go. Take a few days off and go see the doctor.'

Maybe if we do end up in Lockdown, it will give me a chance to stop drinking. I seem to remember Lisa waving some leaflets at me the last time we argued, they must be around here somewhere. I'll have a root around and see if I can find them. There might be something in there to help me because God knows, I need it. Once I straighten myself out, maybe I'll be able to talk to Lisa about Michael

* * *

I opened the front door, already anticipating the first sweet sip of the whiskey from the bottle in my desk drawer. It had been a difficult week and I'd decided, as it was Friday, to give myself a break and come home early. As I passed the partially open living room door a flash of movement caught my eye. Ignoring, for the moment, the siren call of the whiskey, I paused mid-stride and back tracked to the door, being careful not to look inside.

'Why aren't you in school?'

There was a crash and a further flurry of movement. When I considered sufficient time had passed, I stuck my head through the door. Michael glared at me.

'Why aren't you at work?'

'Because I came home early.'

'So did I. Half day.'

'It's not the end of term Michael. Does your mother know you're here?'

This last was directed at the unknown girl whose wide brown eyes were staring at me. She was wearing Michael's school jumper and unruly curls hung over her shoulders as she clutched one of Lisa's oversized cushions to her stomach. She shook her head.

'Then I suggest you get dressed and go home. It's almost the end of school.'

I closed the door behind me and retreated to my office to pour an even larger measure than I'd originally intended. It wasn't the first time I'd been in this situation, but it still required a second drink to steady myself. I couldn't be certain, but I didn't think I'd seen this one before. I could only hope that like Michael, she'd already celebrated her sixteenth birthday. There was a knock at the door.

'She's gone. Will you tell Mum?'

'I won't, but if you keep skipping classes the school will phone your mum. If they do that, I won't lie to her.'

He nodded.

'Message understood.'

I was glad it was. I wasn't sure what message I'd given him and I could already feel the tendrils of a headache beginning to flower and creep their way across my forehead. I didn't need a confrontation that would only allow it to tighten its grip on me. I'd never told Lisa about the previous occasions and I almost certainly wouldn't tell her about this one. She struggled enough with the idea of Michael growing up as it was, always said it reminded her she was getting older as well. She didn't need to know he was skipping school for sex: it would only provoke another evening of laments about how she'd suffered for doing the same. When I'd doused myself in Lynx Africa and strutted off to enjoy those stolen afternoons in Lisa's bedroom, I never gave a thought to consequences beyond the immediate gratification of my desire. She was the one whose education was interrupted, who had to give up her dream of going to university. It was alright for me, I'd already got my degree by the time we got married.

'Why don't you go to university part-time? I'll look after Michael in the evenings while you study. We can just about manage on my salary if we're careful.'

'Don't be ridiculous, Joe! After I've looked after Michael all day the last thing I want to do is start writing essays and besides which, what do you know about looking after him? You never have him on your own.'

'I'll be fine. He's my son too, you know.'

'It's too much when you've been at work all day.'

'If it's something you want to do, I'll manage.'

'It's fine. I've already accepted I won't get a degree.'

No. I definitely wouldn't be telling Lisa.

As he got older, Michael got better at hiding his indiscretions even from me, so it was a shock one day, after he'd started dating Fliss and I'd hoped he was settling down, to find another unknown brunette on her way out of our bathroom. Eyes averted, we exchanged a brief nod before she scuttled back into Michael's room. I took him out for a drink that night.

'Michael... I...' I took a calming breath, trying to ignore

the sweat running down my spine. 'We've all done stupid things after a drink or two. Fliss is a lovely girl and–'

'I was thinking I might look for a place of my own, give you and Mum some space. I've got a bit saved and I thought if I moved out, you guys could do something with my room – a home gym or something? I just think it would be good to be a bit more independent, you know?'

'I do. I think it's a very good idea in fact. Are you going to look for somewhere with Fliss?'

'Maybe. I don't know. To be honest, I might not even do it – I don't know if I'll have a big enough deposit to get somewhere locally – I'm considering it, that's all.'

'Well you'll know all about Help to Buy and if you're a bit short for a deposit, we might be able to give you something.'

'Thanks Dad. You're a legend. Don't say nothing to Mum yet, will you? You know what she's like.'

I did know.

'She'll either be upset that I don't want to live at home no more, or she'll be picking out colour schemes and decorating before I've even found somewhere.'

'That does sound like Mum.'

We laughed, but it was strained. Lisa's moods were unpredictable and it was hard to tell how she was going to react to anything that disturbed her equilibrium. She wasn't the same girl I'd fallen in love with, but I wasn't the same man either. Everyone changes as they age – it's inevitable – but I'd always assumed we'd grow together. Instead, there'd been a steady but inexorable drift apart as I worked longer and longer hours at the office and she shifted from looking after Michael to working part-time and then full-time at the gym. I kept telling myself I'd cut the gruelling hours at work, but somehow it was never the right time – Lisa needed a new car, then she wanted us to have a flash (and therefore expensive) holiday and there were the inevitable school ski trips to pay for and the extra hours I did paid well. For some reason, she could never equate being able to afford the nice things in life with the amount of hours I worked and her resentment of the time I spent at work grew ever larger.

After the conversation in the pub, the flat wasn't mentioned again and although I never saw any of his night-time visitors after that, I heard a few of them creeping down the stairs in the early hours of the morning, but I always made sure not to get up until I heard Michael moving around downstairs. My job was stressful enough without adding further drama to my life and I was conscious that the contents of the whiskey bottle were reducing at an ever-increasing pace. That seductive amber liquid was the one constant in my life now. Most nights she was my first port of call when I arrived home, her voice singing to me even before I'd left work. Only once I'd felt the sting of the first followed by the soothing comfort of the second and the third, did I feel equal to facing the family. It was only with her comforting restfulness flowing through my body that I could keep myself together at the end of a difficult day.

As the pressures of work grew, I knew I was becoming even more distant from both Lisa and Michael. Of course, I was doing the long hours for them – it had always been for them – but that didn't change the fact that we barely saw each other. Consequently, it took me some time to realise that Michael wasn't always coming home after a night out. At first, I assumed he was staying over at Neil's, but once I saw him come home dishevelled and reeking of cigarettes and cheap perfume, I knew where he'd been. I'm ashamed to say it didn't occur to me to wonder how he'd got home. At the time, I was more concerned about it affecting his relationship with Fliss. On numerous occasions I wanted to talk to him about what he was risking, but somehow what started out as Dutch courage ended in slumping over my desk and waking in the early hours of the morning with a stiff neck.

After he died, it only got worse. His death made my failings as a father all the more stark. If I'd spoken to him instead of drinking myself into a stupor, it might have made a difference. I'm sure he'd have listened to me and stopped driving when he was drunk. People laugh about the recklessness of youth, but I know Michael would have taken me seriously. I could have prevented his death and instead, I did nothing.

The knowledge of what I'd done – or rather, not done – bore down on me. I woke most mornings feeling trapped in the bed, the sheets like a medieval *peine forte et dure*. Work was itself another form of torture, pretending to be confident and up to the job, when inside, I alone knew myself for the miserable failure I was. I started having a small one to fortify myself before facing the day, but it didn't help. The crushing knowledge of my failures was still there. One became two, then three. I couldn't face Lisa at the end of a day, didn't want her to suddenly wake up and realise what she was married to. I hadn't even told her I'd been signed off work. If she knew how badly I'd let our son down she'd leave me and rightly so. But I couldn't bear the thought of losing her, so instead I'd go to the pub until I knew she wouldn't want to talk to me and only then would I head unsteadily home.

It was too painful to talk about Michael with her. Every conversation was like a physical wound, so it was easier not to mention him. I hoped that by never talking about him, the image of his body on the slab in the morgue might stop haunting me. Lisa only saw him after the undertaker had seen him, when he looked like our Michael again and I was glad for her. She'd never failed him. She deserved to remember him at his best.

* * *

But now it's time for me to be a man again. The leaflets are in the chest of drawers, angrily crumpled together, but there's something else there as well, hidden in amongst the piles of new underwear. I'm distracted for a moment by the softness of the silk against my fingers and the memory it evokes makes me smile. I draw the box out: it's a pregnancy test. At first I'm delighted. Sex has been sporadic at best in recent months – it's hard to accept your wife finds you attractive when you disgust yourself – but there had been one wonderful evening when the whiskey had whispered to me instead of shouting. Lisa was moved to tears by it and I wasn't so far from weeping myself. How wonderful would it be if that night – made more precious by its rarity – resulted in a fresh start for the two of us? This could be our opportunity, our chance to move on after Michael's death. A new baby would give us something to focus on, to bring us back together. At a time when the world around us was facing its biggest threat in a hundred years, what if spring really had brought forth new life for us?

'We're not too old to do this,' I think. 'Lots of people have babies in their forties.'

I'll have to ask Alan to let me come back to work. We'll need my salary if the Lockdown comes in and even more so if Lisa then has to go on maternity leave. I stop, the smile freezing on my face. What if Alan says no? The thought leaves a nasty taste in my mouth. I tuck the box back into its hiding place and hurry downstairs to my study.

'Just a quick one before I go,' I tell myself. 'I'm good at my job. Alan will give me a second chance. He bloody should do the years I've worked there and the hours I put in.'

My glass is empty. I don't remember drinking it.

'I must have forgotten to fill it,' I think and pour myself a generous measure.

'Just a quick one and then I'll go.'

Shouldn't have been so hard on Neil. Pushed him too far, but who hasn't made mistakes? Paying for it now, ain't I?

NEIL

I can hardly make out what she's saying over the rushing in my ears. My heart is racing and I feel sick. How can this have happened? Well obviously, I know *how*, but how? I never asked, I just assumed, but even so. At her age, I didn't think it would be a problem.

'So I thought I'd do another one while I'm here. Is that OK?'

I nod my head. I need to get out of here.

'I'll go put the kettle on, shall I?'

She frowns, but before she can object, I've pulled my clothes back on and run downstairs, wincing as I stub my bare toe in my haste. As I wait for the kettle to boil I set the mugs out on the counter, then pace up and down the kitchen. There's still hope. If she's doing another test, maybe the first one wasn't a clear result. *How the hell have I ended up in this mess? I never intended for this to happen.*

There's a knock at the door and I throw a worried glance at the ceiling. Even if it's only a delivery driver, everyone knows everyone around here. Still, she'll have the sense not to come down until he's gone.

* * *

I couldn't believe Mike was dead. I kept expecting him to turn up on the doorstep laughing about what a massive trick he'd pulled on us all. When that didn't happen, I half expected his ghost to appear and berate me for not stopping him driving. Any time we got caught, it was always my fault, so why should this time be any different? But what was I supposed to do? When Mike knew he'd pulled, nothing short of a natural disaster was going to prevent him closing the deal. The girl he was with that night had made it pretty clear he was welcome to go home with her and I'd given up warning him about the dangers of drink driving.

'You're so middle-aged Neil. I'm only a bit over the limit, I'll be fine. You know me – best driver to come out of Essex since Alex Albon.

'Alex Albon isn't three sheets to the wind when he's racing round Silverstone though, is he?'

After that, I figured I'd done my best. If I pushed it any further, I knew from experience it would descend into him listing all my shortcomings as a friend and as a man and I wasn't in the mood. I just hoped he didn't take anyone else out with him. Why should he ruin any more lives? He'd spent years ruining mine – I didn't want anyone else to suffer.

Growing up, I was never what you'd call a popular child. I was more interested in books than people; books didn't call me names or throw my lunch in the sandpit. So when I met Mike, I felt like all my prayers had been answered and on the face of it, he was a good mate. He made sure I never got bullied and included me in everything he did, but as with all things, there was a price to pay. The stupid thing is, I don't think he ever meant to make me feel the way he did. He was just joking around, but when you've got an abundance of self-confidence, it's hard to understand how someone who has none takes everything to heart.

'You're such a loser Neil! Just ask her out for God's sake!'

'Nah, course I ain't done the homework! Bet Neil has though. Mr Conscientious!'

When I got my place at university I thought maybe he'd be pleased for me. He knew how much it meant to me.

'Oooo let's see. Where's brainbox off to then? Three As? UCL here you come. At least you'll be able to hang around with us commoners at the weekends though. Assuming of course you still want to associate with us plebs who ain't going to uni?'

As usual, I didn't have much choice in the matter. On my weekends at home and in the holidays it was only natural to drift back into the company I'd kept at school. Mike always seemed to know the second I arrived home and he'd be on the phone arranging a night out.

It was during the long summer break before the start of my final year that we met Fliss. I'd been watching her across the club and timed my trip to the bar so I bumped into her and we started chatting as we waited to be served. We were getting along fine until Mike turned up with his cheesy chat-up line and swept her onto the dancefloor, leaving me holding the drinks. I don't know what surprised me the most, that he was still using the negging technique he'd developed at school, or that it was still successful. His hands were all over her and when he kissed her, I slammed my glass down so hard a thin crack ran up the side of it, but I was impotent. I'd been there so many times before. Once Mike had taken what he wanted, I'd provide a sympathetic ear and occasionally a bit more if it was required. Usually though, by the time they'd recovered from being so unceremoniously discarded, they didn't want anything to do with anyone associated with Mike.

I kept hoping he'd break things off with Fliss: I spent more weekends at home that year than I'd done in the previous two combined and it was all because of her. The more time I spent with her and the more we talked, the more I was convinced she was the one for me. When I came home for good after my finals, I couldn't believe Mike was risking it all by continuing to cheat on her.

'I'm thinking of buying a flat,' he said. 'I dropped a few hints to my dad and he said he'd help with a deposit. You could rent a room off me and we could make it a proper pimp pad. I can get girls for both of us and you might even get laid finally!'

He was so busy laughing at his own joke he didn't see the look of disgust I wasn't quite quick enough to suppress.

'What about Fliss?'

'What about her? She ain't moving in! After how she was this afternoon I ain't even sure I can be bothered with her anymore. She ain't worth the grief.'

He laughed again.

'That why you're still cheating on her?'

'Nah, that's just 'cause I can. Me and her ain't serious.'

'Does she know that?'

That got his attention.

'What she don't know won't hurt her. And it's fuck all to do with you anyway. Just remember whose girlfriend she is, yeah? You're just jealous. I've seen how you look at her, it's pathetic. You can't stand the fact she chose me over you.'

'Would she still want you if I told her what you were really like? About the other girls? Who do you think she'd choose then?'

At first he seemed stunned. In ten years of friendship, I'd almost never argued with him about anything. Then he laughed.

'Go on then. Try it and see. You tell her. But you won't will you Neil? You think you're so much better than me now just 'cause you've been to university and you can talk posh and use long words, but you ain't. You're all mouth and no trousers. Would you even know what to do with a woman if you had one? Cause you never have, have you? Twenty-one and still a virgin. I could hand you Fliss on a plate and you still wouldn't know what to do with her. In fact...I tell you what, that's exactly what I'll do. If you can get Fliss to sleep with you, go for it! Do it with my blessing! Let's see how much of a man you really are.'

I didn't bother telling him I'd been his most faithful student over the years. Why should I tell him that far from being inexperienced, I'd had one-night stands with most of the girls on my course – taken his tactics and refined them, made them my own.

It will just make stealing Fliss away all the sweeter. She was always meant to be mine anyway.

His mood soured after that, so it was almost a relief when he pulled and I could make my excuses and leave.

The next morning, Lisa rang to tell me he was dead.

After the funeral, I kept texting her to make sure she was okay – after all, if I'd kept my mouth shut, we'd never have argued and Mike might still have been alive. I had to do something, especially when a few months later she said she'd been signed off work. I thought flowers and chocolates might cheer her up; that's what Mum always does when her friends are upset. Offering to take her out for the day was the same – it just seemed the right thing to do, but when she asked me why I didn't have a girlfriend I panicked, wondered if she'd realised how I felt about Fliss. I couldn't exactly say, *Because I've been in love with your dead son's girlfriend since the first moment I met her*, so I kept it vague. I was about to add, *Hopefully one day though*, but as I turned my head to speak to her, she was so close I brushed against her lips. I tried to apologise, but then she kissed me and not a little kiss either, it was a full on, tongue down the throat kiss. Mike always said never to look a gift horse in the mouth, so I didn't.

It's Lisa. Your best mate's mum. What are you doing?

All the blood in my body rushed south, swamping my conscience in a tsunami of pure carnal instinct. It had been a while after all. Even before she started feeling for my flies, I knew where we were heading. I tried to suggest moving things upstairs, but she kissed me again before I could get more than a couple of words out. It was pretty clear what she wanted and having a woman be so determined to have sex was a turn on. Most of the girls I'd been with had been quite passive, content to just lay on their backs, so being left in no doubt what she wanted and how she wanted it made me push my conscience aside almost as quickly as she pushed me back against the sofa. There was no longer a question of moving elsewhere and we did it on the sofa, heedless of anyone who might have been passing by. It was quick but good – for a woman her age she was in pretty good shape with a flat stomach and boobs that in the old days we'd have categorised as a BSH – enough to occupy your hands, but not so big you didn't know where to start. She clearly took care of herself and there was something satisfying about not having to pretend I was driven by anything more than gratification. When it was all over it was a bit awkward, so once I'd retrieved my jeans from round my ankles, I made my excuses and left. It was only as I pulled into the driveway at home that I thought about what I'd just done. I'd shagged Mike's Mum. Well, technically I suppose, she'd shagged me, but I'd participated. *Well Mike? You always said I needed to learn from you. Did I learn well?*

I wanted to talk to Lisa about what had happened, but it's hard to open a conversation with, *Hi, nice to see you. Remember the other day when we had sex on your sofa? Well, can we talk about it please?* By the time I'd worked out a way of casually dropping it into conversation, she'd started talking about Mike; how much she missed him, how lovely he was, how Joe was drinking more and more since the funeral. I didn't care. I just wanted to know how she felt about what we'd done. My conscience was beginning to voice its concerns and as much as I tried to ignore it, it was becoming louder.

The Naze was pretty deserted, even for a cold autumn day and low clouds made it look even more desolate than usual, as though all the colour had leaked out of the place. I jammed my fists deep into my coat pocket when Lisa started banging on about Michael again.

'I'm sure he was getting ready to propose.'

No he wasn't.

'I think she might have been the one, you know. I found a load of information about flats in his room and I think he must have been about to ask her to move in with him.'

He wanted a flat so he'd got somewhere to take the girls he met when he went out without Fliss. The flat was nothing to do with her.

'I'm sure marriage wouldn't have been long after that.'

That was the final straw. I had to shut her up. I kissed her, but instantly regretted it. It wasn't enough. I wanted more.

'Sorry. We might be seen.'

It was lame, but better than the truth.

You don't even know what the truth is.

She clearly didn't mind and the memory of her body against mine, sent desire pulsing through me. I pulled her into one of the dilapidated pillboxes, hidden from passers-by, pushed her against the wall and took possession of her again.

What was it about this woman? She was the same age as my mum, but I wanted her so badly I was incapable of controlling myself around her.

My body was acting independently of my brain and once again I was left struggling in its wake. Somewhere along the A12 my conscience finally caught up.

What you're doing is wrong.

I completely agreed, but Mike spent our entire friendship taunting me about my failure with women, so a fling with his mother seemed almost poetic.

Afterwards, Lisa and I continued to snatch all too brief hours together when Joe was at work and I had a day off. Between that and my regular visits to check on Fliss, the weeks flew past and before I knew it, there were Christmas lights in the windows.

On Christmas Eve, I went round to see Fliss. She didn't usually want to talk about Mike – which was fine by me – but that evening she wanted to tell me how much she was missing him.

'I just feel so empty sometimes. I went upstairs this morning and saw the necklace he bought me last Christmas and spent the next hour in tears.'

'He's not worth your tears.'

'What do you mean?'

Did I say that out loud?

'I just meant... he wouldn't want you to be upset.'

'No you didn't. Otherwise you'd have said that. You said he wasn't worth it. What did you mean?'

'I guess I just meant he wasn't the saint everyone's making him out to be.'

'I never said he was a saint. I know Mike had his faults, but I loved him and he loved me.' She looked at me sharply. 'You don't think he loved me?'

'I never said that.'

'No, but your eye twitched.'

'So?'

'Your eye always twitches when someone says something you don't agree with. It's like whenever Mike said he was looking forward to Brexit happening. You never said a word, but your eye always twitched. Did he tell you he didn't love me?'

'Mike? Talk about feelings?'

'Don't evade the question.'

'I'm not. I just —'

'Tell me the truth. Did. He. Love. Me?'

'I...I don't want to speak ill of the dead.'

'Telling the truth isn't speaking ill.'

'I...I don't think he saw your relationship as exclusive. He wasn't ready to settle down yet.'

'So he was shagging around.'

She seemed to deflate, all the fight leaving her.

'I'm such an idiot,' she said quietly.

'Fliss, I —'

'Don't,' she said. 'Don't be nice to me. You'll only make things worse.'

On New Year's Day, she rang and asked if we could go for a drink and at the end of the evening, she kissed me. Kissing Fliss was different to kissing Lisa, like a butterfly after a hurricane. She was soft and gentle, where Lisa was all hard lines and anger and there was an attraction to both. After all those years, after all the quips and snide remarks, both women in Mike's life wanted *me* and I had to admit, it was intoxicating. If this was what it was like for Mike, I could see why he'd found having more than one woman on the go so attractive. I might have had a few girls at university, but none of them ever wanted more. I'd been so caught up in pretending each one was Fliss, I'd never realised this fact until now. The feeling of being wanted, of being desired, made me feel attractive for the first time in my life, but I felt the guilt Mike never seemed to. It was Fliss I really loved of course, but there was something about Lisa, something I couldn't quite put my finger on, that kept drawing me back to her. The sex was good, but it was more than that. At times it scared me how much I wanted her, how much I needed to possess her and that need was something Fliss – no matter how much I loved her – couldn't fulfil. Sex with her, when it finally happened, was disappointing. She was like all the other girls, making the right noises, but passive. This wasn't the Fliss I'd spent over a year fantasising about. That Fliss threw me on the bed and there was a true physical connection between us. There'd been a mistake somewhere. A misstep. She wasn't who I thought she was. But the thing with Lisa had no future either. Maybe it was time to stop trying to be Mike and decide who I wanted to be.

'I was thinking I might leave Joe,' Lisa said one day. 'Things weren't right between us, even before you and now…

well, with everything that's going on, the time seems right to start again.'

'It's a big step. You guys have been married a long time.'

'I know, but I'm still young enough to start again. Have more kids if the man wants them.'

She smiled at me and I knew I needed to speak before she went too far.

'I love our time together Lees, but I've been wondering whether we should cool things down. The last thing I want is to come between you and Joe. Mike wouldn't thank me for splitting his parents up.'

'Please don't leave.' She clung to my arm.' I won't mention leaving Joe again, I promise. We can carry on as we have been. Just come back to bed. Please.'

Her desperation both disgusted and excited me, just as my own need for her induced the same emotions. It was a heady mix and feigning reluctance, I allowed her to pull me back to bed. Afterwards, even as she lay in my arms, I found myself questioning why I wasn't able to break free of her. Every time we had sex it was Fliss I pictured and now that fantasy had become a disappointing reality, I shouldn't have wanted Lisa anymore. Yet I kept coming back. That made me angry and it was her fault. It was Lisa who was to blame for the mess my life had become. I needed to end it and I needed to do it soon.

'I've got a day off on Wednesday, no-one will be at home. Come to mine. Tell Joe you're going shopping or something.'

* * *

It's Fliss. *Dear Lord. Can this afternoon get any worse?*

'Hi gorgeous.' I kiss her cheek. 'What are you doing here?'

'I was just walking past and I saw your car was on the drive. I was going to text and see if you wanted to go to the pub later, but when I saw you were home, I thought I'd knock and ask instead.'

She smiles and tilts her face up. I pull her towards me and oblige her with a kiss, but a second later she goes rigid in my arms. I open my eyes to find hers fixed on a point midway up the stairs. Lisa is standing there in my dressing gown, the pregnancy test in her hand and a smile frozen on her face. Fliss pulls away from me and bolts out of the door. I panic.

'Fliss!'

I wrench open the door she's slammed behind her.

'Fliss, I can explain!'

I'm shouting to an empty street. Already she's out of sight. *What have I done?*

Wish Mum was here. Should've been wearing my seatbelt, but I hate "I told you so's." Sorry Mum. This one ain't your fault.

LISA

I look at my face in the mirror. I notice the sunken hollows in my cheeks are beginning to fill out again and I'm unsure how this makes me feel. My reflection gazes quizzically back at me.

'Not bad for an almost forty-year-old,' 'Not-Lisa' seems to say - this clarifier has taken on greater significance in recent months – then in the next breath she adds, 'But what on earth are you playing at? Women your age just don't do this!'

I have to agree with her sentiments even if we are talking at cross purposes. Middle-aged women don't suddenly embark on a passionate affair with a man young enough to be their son.

At least, I reconsider, thinking of Madonna and Demi Moore, *Not middle-aged women like me; respectable, well brought up, happily married.*

And there it is. The lie I still tell myself. The lie that enables me to take all the guilt and responsibility on myself: happily married. I'd laugh if I wasn't so afraid tears would quickly chase the sound away. Happy. There's nothing happy about my life. Kind and sweet as Neil is, even he doesn't make me happy. He only keeps my mind distracted from the misery for the short time we're together. It's not for long, but those moments in his arms are just enough to keep me from completely slipping into despair. Joe isn't interested in me anymore, so it's been nice to feel wanted, to have been with someone who wants me and who understands about Michael. It all started in those miserable months after the funeral, but it's become so much more complicated since then.

* * *

'I'm sympathetic Lisa, I really am,' Drew said, 'But even you have to admit it doesn't look good to the clients if their trainer keeps weeping all over them.'

It had been just over two months since Michael died and every time I thought I'd cried myself dry, my body found fresh supplies to draw on. My boss was right and deep down I knew it, especially when the doctor agreed with him and signed me off work for three months. I couldn't help feeling I'd failed though. I'd failed Michael by not being there to protect him when he needed me and now I'd failed at work. I didn't just feel like a failure, I was one. Always had been. I'd bunked off school to see Joe, caught up in the heady intoxication of Lynx Africa and illicit sex and as a result, I'd had to give up my plans for university. I couldn't help feeling bitter about my lost opportunity – it was alright for Joe; he'd already graduated when we met and just carried on going to work. It was me who had to deal with all the sickness and the crushed dreams. It was my plans that were interrupted and for what? A man who spent longer and longer at work and never showed any interest in *my* day. Joe might have been the sensible choice at the time, but the sex I'd enjoyed so much in those snatched afternoons had long since petered out, leaving me feeling frustrated and unattractive.

How are you today?

The text pinged just as I arrived home and I dashed off an unguarded response.

Been signed off work for three months. Feeling a bit shit tbh.

Within half an hour Neil arrived at the house bearing a bunch of flowers and a box of chocolates.

'Thought these might cheer you up a bit. You sounded like you were having a bad day.'

'They're beautiful, thank you. Come in for a cuppa?'

I put the flowers in a vase, but their cheerful prettiness only emphasised the cold shabbiness of the rest of the room.

My fingers left holes in the dust on the mantlepiece and I stood for a moment watching the little specks rearrange themselves in the air, forgetting I even had a visitor until Neil pushed a warm mug into my hands. Over the tea, I poured my heart out to him. I'd known him over half his life and it was like talking to Michael again. Joe was about as sensitive as a dead dog and these days he was more interested in the bottom of a bottle than he was in me. I never knew what time he'd be home and when he did get in, he was usually so pissed he wouldn't have noticed if I'd been stark naked and hula hooping. Being told not to go to work was the final straw; work was my escape, somewhere that gave me a chance not to think about things for a while. Now that was gone, all I had to look forward to was sitting around the house on my own, missing my son.

'I can always come round on my days off,' Neil said. 'I'm free on Thursday this week, maybe we could go out for the day? It would get you out of the house at least.'

'You're so sweet.' I wiped away the tears, suddenly desperate for a distraction. 'Why have I never seen you with a girlfriend?'

The abrupt question seemed to startle him into honesty because the reply wasn't what I'd expected. I'd always wondered if he might be gay, had a thing for Michael maybe.

'There is someone, but she's always been unavailable. With someone else, you know? It wouldn't have been right.'

He smiled sadly and I could see the pain in his eyes as he stared at me. My heart broke for him. Poor boy. I couldn't help myself. I stroked his face with the flat of my hand, feeling the rough stubble scratching my palm. I moved to kiss his cheek then something in his eyes made me catch my breath. Did he mean me? There was a moment when I could have stopped it happening. A split second between the hitched breath and when his mouth turned to seek mine. I could have backed away but I didn't. His lips brushed against mine. Instantly he pulled back.

'Sorry...I —'

'Don't apologise, it's OK.'

I pulled his head down and returned the kiss. I could feel his initial hesitation, but then he deepened the kiss and I groaned. It had been a long time and I could feel the desire I'd suppressed for so long surging through my body. I'd tried so hard to get Joe to show an interest in me, to recapture the closeness we'd once shared, even resorting to dreaming up a new persona for the bedroom. 'Not-Lisa' was everything I wasn't: confident, sexy, bold, sure of what she wanted. It made no difference to Joe, but I unleashed something (or someone) in myself I'd thought was lost forever. It had been hard to let her out of the box she'd been in and it was proving harder still to push her back in. Now she'd got a taste of freedom she wasn't going to relinquish it without a fight. I caught the scent of Neil's aftershave as we squirmed into a more comfortable position and the familiarity of it brought me almost to tears. Twenty years on, Lynx Africa was still popular and still had the power to make my insides melt. I groaned again – was it desire or despair? – and surrendered my body to 'Not-Lisa', unable to fight her any longer. Neil didn't seem to know what to do with his hands, but 'Not-Lisa' was content to direct them to where they needed to be and at first, he seemed happy for her to take the lead, but when her fingers fumbled for his flies, he grabbed them.

'Lisa, I—'

'Sshh. It's fine. Joe won't be home for hours.'

It didn't last long and when I came to myself, the guilt was excruciating, but it was the first time I'd had sex anywhere except in a bed and the release was wonderful. I'd poured all my hurt and anger into that moment, letting it lose itself in the passion and for a brief time I felt lighter than I had done for weeks. It was wrong on so many levels, but to my shame, I found I didn't care. For once it was just about me.

I spent the next few days swinging between guilt and exultation, but even when I tried again and again to encourage him, Joe continued to show no interest in me, other than occasionally asking when dinner would be ready. Except that is, for the one night I caught him just at the right moment – between drinks five and six – and he allowed me to lead him upstairs. There were no words exchanged and I doubt he noticed the tears, but it was something at least.

Thursday came and with it, the promised day out. I'd had no contact with Neil since that afternoon and I wasn't sure whether the proposed trip would go ahead, or whether he regretted what had happened. However, he turned up promptly at ten o'clock.

'I thought we'd go for a walk at Walton and then go somewhere for lunch.'

It was clear he didn't want to talk about what we'd done, so instead, we talked about Michael. Joe didn't want to talk about him at all. It was almost as though he wanted to pretend our son had never existed, but I didn't. I wanted to talk to someone who'd known Michael, someone with whom I could share my memories and my grief. Neil was happy to listen.

'He was such a wonderful son,' I said. 'And you know what a good friend he was. He never caused me any upset even as a teenager. We were so lucky with him and then when he brought Fliss home, we knew she was the one. I'm sure he was getting ready to propose. I found a load of information about flats in his room and I think he must have been about to ask her to move in with him. I'm convinced marriage wouldn't have taken long after that.'

He didn't say anything.

'Hey,' I nudged him. 'You OK?'

Suddenly, I found myself in his arms, being thoroughly

kissed, every sense alert. The wind whipping through my hair, the sea flexing its muscles, pulling at the sand on the beach below us. Everything was wild and out of control, raw power crackling in an electric storm of emotion and 'Not-Lisa' threw herself directly into the heart of it. Allowing us both to be carried by the raging wind she threw her head back, laughing at and revelling in the tempest, while I was dragged along behind her, my whispered protests unheard beneath the roar of the thunder. Then he released me just as abruptly and I felt bereft.

'Sorry. We might be seen.'

I looked around the windswept brushland with its carved wooden sculptures and laughed, still caught up in 'Not-Lisa's' enjoyment of the giddiness of being out of control. 'I don't think the woolly mammoth statue will tell.'

Just around the corner was an old World War Two pillbox and it was to there he dragged me, pulling me into the cold underground interior and pushing me up against the graffitied concrete, unzipping his flies and pulling up my skirt almost in one movement.

'That's better.' His hands were cold against my warm skin and I flinched as the rough surface of the wall scoured the flesh of my back.

After lunch we drove home and I invited him in. This time we made it as far as the bedroom.

Over the next few months, I found myself constantly anticipating the buzz of my phone, excitable as a schoolgirl when a message appeared. 'Not-Lisa' thought my newly discovered eagerness was funny and pathetic in equal measure. She enjoyed the freedom it gave her but despised me for the weakness she saw in me.

Leaving work early. See you soon x

His entry into the house was always very sedate and conscious of the neighbours, but once inside, it was a different story. Although he was always sensitive and sweet, I began to discover he had hidden depths. His inexperience still showed at times, but on the whole, having a younger lover was definitely to be recommended. I had my confidence back and I even wore the new underwear I'd originally bought to tempt Joe. Neil was far more appreciative of it. I also briefly looked into what my situation would be, financially speaking, if I left Joe. I reckoned I was still young enough – just – to start again and I tentatively raised the subject, purely as a hypothetical, to see if I was being ridiculous.

'I love our time together, Lees, but I've been wondering whether we should just cool things down. You're married and the last thing I want is to come between you and Joe. Mike wouldn't thank me for splitting his parents up.'

'Please don't leave.' Coming out of the blue as it had done, it was a shock and loathing myself for my weakness, I was desperate for it not to end. I was rediscovering life and the thought of having it snatched away was terrifying. 'I won't mention it again. I didn't mean I'd leave him for you. I only meant I was thinking of starting again on my own. I don't expect anything more from you than what we have now. We can carry on as we have been. Just come back to bed. Please.'

I could tell his heart wasn't really in it, but he soon warmed up and at least for a while, I managed to avoid thinking about what I now understood was the inevitable outcome of the affair. I'd been a fool to think I could hold onto this forever, but at least I could withdraw with my dignity intact. Maybe the Lockdown everyone was predicting was a sign this would come to its natural conclusion. After all, Neil and I wouldn't be able to meet if we weren't allowed to leave our own homes.

Perhaps this was the best way. After all, Joe and I didn't have a bad life together. We'd been happy in the beginning when he was everything I wanted. I was ambitious and so was he – we were going to conquer the world together and then Michael happened. And then the accident. We'd intended to have more children, but how could I have more when I couldn't look after one properly? It wasn't even as if I'd been arguing with Michael about something important. He wanted sweets and I said no. He had a paddy and his flailing arm caught the wire of the iron. I'll never forget that scream. After that, I refused to contemplate another child – what if I was distracted by the baby and something happened to Michael? I couldn't risk another accident.

Over the next few days I kept asking myself the same questions. *Do you want this to end? Is there really any chance for you and Joe?* But despite their frequent repetition, by the time I next saw Neil I was no closer to being able to answer them.

'What is it about you that keeps me coming back?' Neil sounded angry and I pulled the sheet around me before sitting up.

'What do you mean?'

'I can't keep away from you! I tell myself to end it and then the next minute I find myself outside your door, praying you'll let me in.'

I felt the need to be honest. 'Not-Lisa' sulked but I ignored her.

'I feel the same. We have to stop this.'

'We do.'

We stared at each other for a long moment. Then between frantic kisses soured by desperation, he gasped out,

'I've got a day off on Wednesday. No-one else will be at home. Come to mine. If Joe's at home, tell him you're going shopping or something.'

In the end, I didn't need to make an excuse, Joe was quiet all morning and then he locked himself in his study. I assumed he was drinking in there and told myself I didn't care. It meant I was free to leave without making an excuse. There was something I needed to talk to Neil about and it couldn't be put off.

* * *

I tear my gaze away from the mirror. Surely three minutes is up now. I look down at the two small windows on the stick in front of me. This time, the result is clear. I smile and look back at the mirror. 'Not-Lisa' has disappeared and all I see is the old me staring back at me. Wrapping Neil's dressing gown tighter around my body, I run out of the bedroom towards the stairs.

'I've got the result,' I shout, waving the stick in the air as I descend.

Fliss is standing with him at the bottom of the stairs. *When did she arrive? I didn't even hear anyone knock, let alone hear Neil open the front door.* She stares at me and I stare back. My mouth opens and I close it again. I don't know what to say. She turns, wrenches the door open and runs out into the street.

'Fliss, wait!'

My phone vibrates. I look down at it, don't recognise the number and go to kill the call, but at the last minute something makes me answer it.

'Lisa? It's Alan. I'm afraid I've got some bad news for you. Joe's been taken to hospital with a suspected heart attack. They've asked if you can meet them there.'

I look at Neil and wonder who I've been these past few months.

'I've got to go.'

Fliss. Lovely Fliss. Nice girl. Probably didn't treat her as good as I should've, but that's life innit? Don't always get what you deserve. I don't deserve this.

FLISS

She comes to me again in the early hours of the morning when she knows I'm normally at my most vulnerable.

It was never going to last anyway. None of your relationships do. People like you don't deserve to be happy. It's your own fault, you know. You could have carried on in blissful ignorance if you hadn't been so selfish. If you'd agreed to go out with them that night he'd still be here, but no, you needed to work. If you'd put him first, he'd be alive and you'd still think he loved you. You brought it on yourself.

I shake my head, trying to dislodge her, but she's wrapped tightly around me now and it's like trying to remove ivy.

'You can't live your life by "what ifs",' I tell her, parroting my counsellor. 'The accident wasn't my fault.'

You were being a bad girlfriend.

'He was a worse boyfriend.'

He'd have listened to you and got a taxi.

'Is that the best you've got? We both know that's not true. Besides, I had to work. Seb wanted my opinion on the submissions by the next morning.'

You put work before your boyfriend and he died as a result.

'No. He died because he was driving drunk after cheating on me.'

You're not good enough to keep any man, are you? Even your dad had enough in the end.

I wrap a pillow around my ears, trying to drown her out, but still she persists, whispering her poison into my ears. In the end I give up and switch my light on. Maybe if I get up and get on with some work she'll get bored and leave me alone. I should know by now not to try reasoning with her – The Voice has been my constant companion for as long as I can remember – but I still hope that one day I'll defeat her. My latest counsellor has suggested some new techniques and sometimes they work for a little while. Distracting myself is one of them, so I start up my laptop and fire off a quick text to Seb letting him know I'll be working from home today. Almost immediately my phone pings in reply.

No problem. You OK? Here if you need a chat. S x

I make it through until after lunch and then she comes back.

Didn't take you long to move on either, did it? He's only been dead a few months and you've already got yourself a replacement. Not exactly the loving faithful girlfriend you portray yourself as, are you?

'He wasn't exactly faithful to me!' I remind her.

You've only got Neil's word for that. Mike always said he fancied you, didn't he? Didn't take him long to make a move after Mike died, did it?

'It's not like that. I just feel a bit sorry for him. He had to watch me with Mike for so long when he wanted me himself.'

Why would he want you? Why would anyone? You're nothing special. He'll drop you in an instant just like all the others and why wouldn't they? Look at you. You're fat, you're ugly and you're boring. Who wants to be lumbered with that?

'I'm not listening to you.'

I only have to survive until Mum comes home from work. When I'm with her, The Voice sulks. She knows she can't get at me when Mum's there because in a battle of wills, Mum never loses. She's a force to be reckoned with and The Voice is powerless in the face of that, so she's mostly given up even trying.

Maybe if I go for a walk I can leave her at home? I get my coat and head out into the cold.

* * *

Dad walked out on us when I was seven. Simply came home one day and announced he didn't love either of us, packed his bag and left. I haven't seen him since that day, so it's always been just me and Mum. She's my best friend and I wouldn't have made it this far in life without her. Most mums sit outside ballet studios and swimming pools, but not mine. Mine sat outside one counsellor's office after another as I saw a succession of them throughout my childhood and teenage years. One after another they'd pronounce their sessions had worked. I'd talked through the trauma of Dad leaving and demonstrated I could make adequate use of the coping strategies they'd given me for when The Voice reared her head. I'd agree with their diagnosis and then a few years later I'd relapse and have to start again with a different one. The counsellors came and went, but Mum was always there waiting at the end of a session and we'd go for a hot chocolate (or two if the conversation was long enough). She never asked me to talk to her about the sessions, but I did anyway. I loved that she knew me well enough to let me do and say things in my own time.

The Voice never fully went away, but I got better at shutting her up as I got older, or at least, I learned not to listen to everything she said. I ignored her mocking comments when I went for an interview at a small independent publishing company and got the job of Junior Editor.

I don't know why you're so happy. It's a grand title but you're basically just the office dogsbody. You'll be making coffee all day.

I did make a lot of coffee, but most of it was for me and I loved my job. There were only a handful of us in the office and we all got on really well. Some of the manuscripts I picked out made it through the final selection and I was praised for having spotted their potential from within the slush pile. Seb was a brilliant mentor as well as my boss and he was happy to spend hours after work talking to me about the job, the manuscripts I'd looked at that day, life and everything else besides. He even suggested I start going to book launches and pitching meetings with him to get more experience.

The Voice sulked. When things were going well she had less to say that could rattle me and she didn't like it.

The night I met Mike however, she was having a great time. I'd agreed to go out with some old school friends and I'd been drinking – never a good move for me – it gave her freedom to say what she pleased. It was precisely why I wasn't normally a big drinker. I went to the bar to get more vodka in an attempt to drown her out and bumped into Neil. He introduced himself and we got chatting. When he found out I worked in publishing we started talking about the books we'd read and she went away in a huff, knowing this was one area she couldn't touch me on.

'If your face was as lovely as your legs, I'd have to marry you tomorrow.'

I was conscious of a firm body pressed against my back and his breath was hot on my ear, but even at that proximity, the vodka made me uncertain I'd heard him correctly. I wasn't sure if I'd been complimented or insulted and my hesitant confusion gave Mike the opportunity to pull me away from the conversation and onto the dancefloor. I wasn't overly pleased at first: I'd been enjoying talking to Neil, but then I saw his face and I no longer cared.

'I'm Mike.'

'Felicity. But my friends call me Fliss.'

'Hi Fliss.' He grinned.

He was gorgeous. Way out of my league.

Everyone's out of your league.

'I know that. Don't rub it in.'

He's only after one thing, you know. S-E-X.

'Well he's not getting it from me, so shut up.'

You fancy him though, don't you? Everyone else is doing it, but not you. You're too scared.

She was right. I was. Not of the act itself – I knew the mechanics of it and they didn't worry me too much – of letting my guard down and getting hurt. I wasn't in any rush to give her more sticks to beat me with. I didn't sleep with him that night, but when to my surprise, he actually used the phone number I'd given him, we went out again and it didn't take many dates before I allowed things to progress further.

Naturally, Mum was concerned and in her usual careful way, let me know she thought things were moving too fast.

'I'm OK, Mum, honestly! I know it's not been long, but he's fun to be with. Even she's piped down recently.'

After that, even Mum came to love Mike. Anyone who banished The Voice was all right by her.

Mike made me feel as though I was the centre of his universe. He ordered for me when we went out for dinner, bought me clothes he thought would suit me and warned me to be careful not to give Seb the wrong impression. I had no idea I'd been flirting with my boss and Mike knew I'd hate to jeopardise the job I loved. If I went out without him he always rang to make sure I was home safely and to say goodnight. I felt loved.

Ironically, the only time we ever argued was the day he died. I came home from work with a stack of manuscripts to read because it was too noisy to concentrate in the office and I knew I'd have a good few hours before Mum came home. Mike turned up about ten minutes after I'd got in.

'What are you doing home?'

'I wanted somewhere quiet to read these.' I indicated the stack of paper on my desk. 'How did you know I was home anyway?'

'I was on my way to a viewing and I saw your car.' He looked away, his gaze focused on my bookshelf.

'Well I could really do with getting on.' I smiled and gave him a gentle push. 'Technically I am still at work.'

'Boring.' He yawned. 'Come out tonight.'

'I can't, I told you. I've got to read these.'

'So you're putting work before me? Some girlfriend you are.'

I started to laugh, thinking he was joking, but his face was stony and the laughter died almost before it left my mouth.

'You know I'd prefer to be with you, but I really have got to get through these.'

He pulled his arm away from the conciliatory hand I'd stretched out.

'No you wouldn't. You'd rather read this load of shite than have fun with me. God you're as bad as Neil!'

Told you he'd get bored of you, The Voice crowed.

I stayed silent.

'It's pathetic. I mean, look at the state of this one!' Mike plucked a book off the shelf and waved it at me.

'Put that back.'

'It's a tatty old kid's book. You're twenty-one – bit old for that kind of thing ain't you?'

He laughed and waved it again. Three of the loose pages fluttered out.

'I said put it back!'

I tried to snatch the book out of his hand, but he held it out of reach.

'Get out.'

'What?'

'Get out!'

I'd never spoken to him like that before.

'You're mad, you are. It's only a bloody book!'

The book bounced off the wall and thirty seconds later the front door slammed. I didn't care. I was too busy slotting the fallen pages back into their rightful places, fingers shaking.

That book was one of my most treasured possessions and no one except me was allowed to touch it. On the rare occasions I re-read it, I used the newer copy that stood next to it on the shelf, so desperate was I not to damage it further.

Wind in the Willows. Never had one book - not the story but the physical book itself, now battered and bent almost beyond recognition - meant so much to me. Between its thin cardboard covers it encompassed so much of my childhood self: stubborn, unable to see beyond the obvious but by its end, awakened to a whole new world of literary possibilities. It was the first bedtime book Mum tried to read to me after Dad left and I had instantly dismissed it as boring. At seven I didn't understand anthropomorphism, didn't want to understand it. I was too occupied with being upset and angry to even think about it. Being told what a wonderful book it was only made me dig my heels in further.

'I don't want you to read it.'

Mum said nothing and quietly tucked it away on the shelf, lips pressed together tightly as she selected another book instead.

Some little while later though, she informed me she'd bought tickets for us to go and see a production of it in the local park. I didn't want to go and yet, as the day grew closer, I found myself being infected by Mum's excited anticipation and even, to my horror, began just a little, to look forward to it myself.

That night was one of those wonderful drawn-out summer evenings that never seem to end, the sun taking its time to cross the last few inches of sky before sinking reluctantly below the horizon, leaving a lingering warmth in the air as a faint reminder of its existence. We followed the cast around the park; deep into a shady glen to the Wild Wood, high on the hill to Toad Hall, beside the placid lake for the River and onto a path for the frenetic activity of the Railway and the Road. Never before or since had I felt such unadulterated joy in a performance, the exhilaration of moving with the action, of being a part of the scenery, observing it from outside and experiencing it from within, all at the same time. I came away in awe of everything I'd seen and with such a deep, desperate, burning desire to read the book, I could barely wait to get home and begin. Not once did Mum say, 'I told you so'; not when I delayed going to bed that night to begin reading it, not when she found not one, but *four* copies of it on my bookshelf and not even when she found me, years later, sobbing in my bed at two in the morning, reading the devastating conclusion of the follow-up series. She just smiled and tucked me back into bed.

Nobody touched that book.

When I got the phone call from Lisa the next day, The Voice was in her element, repeating the argument over and over again, Hecate-esque in her glee. Macbeth's triad had nothing on her when she sensed blood.

I knew you'd find a way to screw things up, but even by your standards this is pretty spectacular. Actually killing your boyfriend over a book is quite a feat.

'It's not your fault, sweetheart,' Mum said, stroking my hair. 'You can't blame yourself for Mike's poor decision making.'

'But if I'd just been with him,' I sobbed.

'Then you might have been dead as well and I'd be grieving for you as well. I'm very glad you weren't.'

'Well I'm not! I wish I'd been with him!'

'You don't mean that darling.'

But I did. The Voice had been telling me for years I'd be better off dead and maybe she was right. She'd been right about everything else after all. At Mum's insistence, I started seeing yet another counsellor. This one told me I was suffering from survivor's guilt, but she was wrong. I didn't feel guilty to be alive when Mike wasn't, I simply wanted to join him in death. Without him the world had turned very dark again and The Voice was starting to make sense. She was the voice of reason, confirming what I'd always thought; the world would be a better place without me in it. Mum's life would certainly be easier with no messed-up daughter to worry about. She'd be upset at first, but then she'd move on with her life free from stressing about me all the time. Without me to think about, she might even find herself a man to make her happy. She'd be able to put herself first for once.

In one of my more rational moments, I set myself the target of making it as far as the funeral. I needed to say goodbye to Mike and I wanted the opportunity to tell the world how much he meant to me. I went to see him a few days before, to apologise for shouting at him. I couldn't bear the thought of him dying, worrying that I was angry with him, maybe thinking I didn't love him anymore. That was almost worse than the thought he'd died all alone.

After the funeral, I started stockpiling the sleeping tablets I'd persuaded the doctor to give me. I didn't have a specific plan as such, they were more of an insurance in case I decided I wanted them. Everyone did their best to help. If I was in the office, Seb would casually appear with coffee and stop for a chat. If I was working from home Mum and Neil would text throughout the day to check I was still alive. They said they were just checking I was okay, but I knew what they were really doing and it made no sense. I was more likely to do it on a day I was going to work.

Stepping out in front of a train would be messy, but it would get the job done. You're too much of a coward to take sleeping pills or slit your wrists. You've been on the internet. You've seen the statistics. If you're going to do it, do it properly, don't make a half-hearted attempt at it. You've read the advice online, use it.

When it came out exactly how and where Michael died, all Mum's doubts about him resurfaced.

'What was he even doing there at that time in the morning? The clubs all close by three, so what was he doing in Chelmsford until gone four? Something's wrong somewhere. They've not told you the whole story.'

'Stop it. Just stop it. I know what you're suggesting and you're wrong. He was probably getting food or something.'

'For an hour and a half? Where?'

It was a question I couldn't answer and much as I tried to ignore it, it nagged away at me.

You know he was with someone else, don't you? You know it and you don't want to admit it.

'He wasn't like that. He loved me and you can't bear the fact he shut you up for a while.'

You keep telling yourself that if it makes you feel better, but you know it's not true. It's the only explanation that makes sense. He didn't love you any more than your dad did. You were so desperate to be loved you ignored the signs. How many times did he go out without you? Didn't even ask if you wanted to go? And you're such an idiot that even now you're pining for someone who didn't give two hoots about you. It's pathetic. You're pathetic.

She wouldn't be silenced and in the end, just before Christmas, I asked Neil.

'Do you know where he'd been that night?'

'I told you, I went home on my own at about two. He was having a good time, but I'd had enough. I don't know where he went after I left.'

'Was he with someone else maybe? Could he have gone on to a party somewhere? I'm sorry,' I said as the tears began to fall. 'I just miss him so much. This morning I found a necklace he'd bought me and I spent the next hour in tears.'

'He's not worth your tears.'

I thought at first I might have misheard him, but one look

at Neil's face convinced me I hadn't. It took some arm twisting, but eventually I got the truth out of him. The Voice had been right all along. Mike never loved me, not in the way I'd loved him. We'd been together for a year and I'd thought it was as serious for him as it was for me. We were only young but Mike had talked about marriage – I hadn't imagined that – but it seemed it was all part of whatever game he was playing. I'd fallen for every one of his lies and worse, I'd never questioned any of them. She had. She'd known all along. She kept telling me and I refused to listen, stupidly confident in the strength of my relationship. I was an idiot.

'You know I've always cared about you, Fliss. Mike never deserved you. If you'd been my girlfriend I'd never have behaved like that. I saw you first that night – went out of my way to talk to you, but then Mike swooped in and that was it.'

'I always assumed it was just that you liked talking about books, but Mike always joked about you having a crush on me. He thought it was hilarious. I thought he was just having a laugh, but he knew didn't he? He knew how you felt and he was rubbing it in your face. Why did he tell me though? Was it some kind of test, to see if I showed any signs of preferring you? Was he hoping I would so he could justify his own behaviour?'

'I don't know. It wasn't something we talked about.'

'I'm such an idiot. I thought he loved me, but it was the control he loved, wasn't it?'

'Fliss, I —'

'Don't.' I put my finger over his lips. 'Don't be nice to me. You'll only make things worse.'

I made him leave, but I spent the next few days thinking about what he'd said and I decided I wasn't going to spend any more time mourning the Mike I thought I'd lost. He'd never existed except in my imagination. Meanwhile, there was a very real man who wanted me, who'd been in love with me for a year and never said a word because I was with his best mate. A man who willingly gave up his free time to look after his friend's mother while she grieved for her son – not many men of his age would have done that. He wasn't the man for me – too serious by far – but I wanted, no needed, to be with someone I knew found me attractive and I knew sleeping with Neil would have seriously pissed Mike off, which made the idea all the more appealing.

My decision made, I threw the photo of Mike into the drawer of my bedside table and slammed it shut, hearing the sound of breaking glass with a sense of quiet satisfaction. Then I called Neil and suggested going for a drink. At the end of the evening I kissed him and suggested another date. It wasn't the same as kissing Mike; he'd been all fire and passion and with Neil it lacked any spark, but it was safe. Part of me enjoyed the feeling of being on the edge, the element of danger with Mike; it was exciting and hypnotic, but I'd been burned by it and I wanted something less passionate, but more reassuring.

The first time we slept together I was pleasantly surprised. Mike had always made a joke about Neil's lack of experience in the bedroom, but it seemed that was another thing my late boyfriend was wrong about. Unless he was an exceptionally quick learner, Neil was clearly more experienced than Mike gave him credit for. It wasn't enough though and once the satisfaction of picturing Mike's reaction wore off, I knew it was never going to work. Revenge was not a good basis for a long-term relationship.

It was all very well my deciding I was no longer going to mourn for or feel guilty about Mike, but it was another thing entirely to persuade my mind to do as it was told. Consequently, whilst I'd enjoyed the brief respite from The Voice, it wasn't long before she slunk back, hiding between my thoughts and then emerging when I least expected her.

When are you going to learn? You can't hold onto a man. He'll let you down like all the others. You'll never be enough.

I wanted to tell her that said more about them than it did me, but I couldn't be bothered to argue with her. I didn't know what else I wanted, I just knew I was tired of the constant fight to prove myself worthy.

* * *

Once I'm out in the fresh air, I feel better. Her voice isn't as loud out here: she's drowned out by the noise of life carrying on about its business. I'm not really thinking about where I'm going, I'm just desperate to put some distance between me and her and when I wake to my surroundings, I find I'm walking past Neil's house. His car is on the drive and I realise he must have come home early from work. I don't want to be at home, I need some breathing space away from her for a while, so I decide to see if he wants to go to the pub this evening.

He seems distracted when he lets me in and I realise I've probably disturbed him when he was about to have a shower, as his feet are bare and his clothes dishevelled. Still, he seems pleased to see me. It's only as he's kissing me that I realise there is someone else in the house. I stare as Michael's mum appears on the stairs. It takes me a moment to register that she's wearing Neil's dressing gown and she has a pregnancy test in her hand.

Told you so.

'Fliss —'

Before he can complete his excuse, I'm out of the house and running down the street, the door slamming shut behind me.

The Voice says nothing. She doesn't have to. I can feel her smugness radiating through me.

AMELIA

The minute I walk through the door I can tell something is wrong. The house doesn't feel right. Fliss said she was working from home today and usually the radio is on, but today there's nothing except a cold stillness. Fliss' phone is on the table and it beeps.

I'm so sorry. J had heart attack. On way to hospital now. Will call l8r. L x

I race upstairs shouting her name. She comes out of the bathroom, her face pale.

'Hello, you're home early,' she says.

'I thought...never mind...I...'

She looks confused for a moment, then her face clears.

'Why are men such losers, Mum?'

She throws her arms around me and I feel her shoulders shaking. I automatically go to comfort her, but then it slowly dawns on me. She's laughing. I'm not sure if it's amusement or hysteria.

'Oh Mum,' she says. 'I'm so glad you're home. We need to talk, but I think it might call for two hot chocolates.'

I smile.

Sirens? Too late. Too tired. So much pain. So scared. Darkness when there should be daylight. Rain coming? Final indignity, dying in the pissing rain.

About the Author

Ruth's first writing memory is for her writer's badge in Brownies but her MA in Creative Writing probably trumps that. Ruth is the co-founder and director of the publishing company Castle Priory Press and has been Writer In Residence at Brightlingsea Lido since 2021. Ruth publishes adult books under her own name and children's books under the pen name Henrietta Edwards. Ruth has also been published in various anthologies, helping to edit many of them as well. Ruth's next book for adults, 'Blythewode' is planned for release later in 2023.

Also by R. E. Loten

Unforgettable

Folly

The Reign Of The Winter King (as Henrietta Edwards)

Max, The Brightlingsea Cat (as Henrietta Edwards

'Unforgettable'

There are first loves and there are last loves. But what happens when they overlap?

Tom Blythe falls in love quickly. He fell for Olivia the first time they met. The same thing happens when he meets Grace. The problem is: Tom is still in love with Olivia.

Pulled in two different directions, Tom has a choice to make. He knows he's unhappy, but is that enough for him to forget the vows he made? Both women have difficult pasts and Tom is desperate to help them, but at what cost?

Can he let Olivia go and commit his future to Grace? Or will the pull of the past prove too strong?

PROLOGUE

I'll always remember the first day I saw *her*; the woman who made me, at least temporarily, forget that I had been married to the woman I loved for ten wonderful years. She was reading a book and I think that's what caught my attention to be honest. Such a large book in the hands of so slight a person. The solemn looking tome looked out of place in such a vibrant setting, out of context with both its surroundings and its owner.

She lifted her head and blinked, as dazed by the sun as I was by her. Our eyes met and a brief half smile flashed across her face in acknowledgement of the contact; for that moment I was lost. Lost to myself, lost to every sense of moral propriety I had ever held dear; lost to my wife; lost to everything save HER.

PART ONE: OLIVIA 1997

At the age of eighteen, I had been deemed mature enough to begin making my own life choices. Fulfilling every cliché going, I cast off the guiding hand of my parents, declared myself an independent, free spirit and selected a university that was far enough from home to allow me to demonstrate this.

I was going to be a new person. Until now, I'd been quite insular in my outlook on life – in some ways I was fairly streetwise, but in others I'd been told I was hopelessly naïve. Unlike many of my peers, I didn't leave behind me a string of abandoned girlfriends. My parents were quite old-fashioned and I guess some of their views rubbed off on me. I wasn't interested in one night stands – if I'm being perfectly honest, I was more interested in women in a theoretical way. Frankly, the reality of them scared me. I'd been brought up to be respectful of them – love was something to be cherished, not a fleeting physical act. The girls I'd known however, viewed themselves differently – they didn't necessarily want to be looked after and my female classmates had set about re-educating me to some extent.

I knew I was a work in progress, but I was optimistic about this chance for a fresh start. I would consider the well-meant advice they'd given me and attempt to put it into practice. No one in Exeter knew the old me and I was determined that my new personality would be a success.

It wasn't that I disliked my home city (or my family) so much that I had to move away, or even that I particularly wanted to prove I could be a different person. It was simply a logical and calculated choice to study at the best university for my course. Exeter had an outstanding reputation. Its distance from home and the subsequent feeling of independence, were nothing more than an added bonus.

Consequently, I found myself standing outside a crumbling manor house, its cream paint peeling and flaking away to reveal the brickwork beneath. It seemed a fitting and slightly depressing reminder of the house's faded stature: from grand home of the at least rich, if not famous, to an accommodation block for a hotchpotch of students, some of whom would have been more likely to be found in the servants' quarters in the house's heyday.

Not that it wasn't attractive in its own way; it certainly had character and the grounds were beautiful – a rolling landscape of wide paths and lush gardens. At the bottom of the garden sat thickly foliaged plants that would – as we later discovered - give you a nasty looking rash if you so much as breathed too heavily near them.

Unfortunately, none of this mattered to me, not only

because I knew nothing of plants and had little to no appreciation of the beauty that surrounded the house, but also because, as I was soon informed, I was not to be housed in it. The property had been gifted to the university on the proviso that no male students were to be allowed to reside in the main house. Modern equality laws being what they were, the university had, in its wisdom, decided that this stipulation was not really practical and got around the clause by housing male students in what had at one time been the stables and the Lodge House. Thus, the hall could still be mixed accommodation. It was to the latter building – now referred to as 'Westgarth', or more colloquially, 'the Garth' – that I was assigned. With a handful of other, equally disgruntled looking young men, I made my way there, dragging almost all my worldly possessions behind me along the uneven gravelled path. My battered old case bounced madly behind me, its wheels – damaged on a recent family holiday to France – squeaking maniacally as though the very notion of turning was torturous to them.

Having been shown to my room by the Deputy Hall Warden (a tall, miserable-looking PhD student, who informed us in a surly voice, that his name was Reece and he sincerely hoped we would not cause him any trouble this year) I paused for a moment, my hand on the door handle. I was suddenly unwilling to open it and meet the person who would be my room-mate for the next year. Having been part of the same group of friends from my early teens, the idea of now having to make new ones was a little alarming. I'm not normally given to these moments of introspection so it came as a nasty shock to find I was actually quite nervous.

Mentally giving myself a shake, I took a deep breath, in part just to assure myself I could, then pushed the handle down and the door open. The cold metal froze the ready smile to my face as I determined to make the best of whatever was on the other side. I was glad I'd taken those moments to steady myself because my first impressions were not positive ones. My room-mate was an anxious looking boy with a thin, pinched face. He barely lifted his eyes from his book when I entered the room, rheumy blue eyes behind thick lenses completing the unprepossessing features. I forced myself to speak.

'Hi, I'm Tom.'

'Hello,' he muttered. 'Peter.'

I appeared to be of little interest to him, so I crossed the room and dumped my case on the bed. Then, under the guise of arranging my own possessions, I surreptitiously observed him as he sat hunched over the desk.

The light from the functional white desk lamp spilled over its surface, illuminating the gathering gloom of the late September afternoon and casting a hunchbacked shadow onto the wall behind it. Spidery handwriting already filled several of the pages that were strewn across the desk and the text in the book was highlighted with scribbled notes crammed into both margins. I was reminded of an illustration I'd seen of Doctor Frankenstein at work creating his monster and smiled at how fanciful I was becoming. I imagined that somehow, the mere fact of having arrived in this hall of learning meant I was suddenly filled to the brim with new and exciting knowledge. I had a new and improved understanding of the world around me. I was now truly, indeed, a *student*: full of the same feelings of hope and optimism that had swept the country a few months earlier. The General Election had seen the first change of government for eighteen years. The new Prime Minister had swept to power on a tidal wave of support from people disillusioned with years of grey, uninspiring leadership. With his appointment, the Houses of Parliament seemed to be infused with sudden, spectacular colour. 'Things Can Only Get Better' reflected my parents' sense of buoyancy after years of floating rudderless, along a narrow blue river on which the wealthy sailed. The same wealthy who ignored those who fell off the ship and drowned under negative equity, unemployment and a whirlpool of debt. My parents were excited at the thought of change. I'd seen the new wave of women MPs greeted with joy by female friends who felt they were finally being given a voice in the halls of power. Only now did I fully understand that thrill, that sense of something have arrived, of being at the start of a brave new world. My daydream ground to a halt with this cliché and my smile became wry as I realised that perhaps there was still some work to be done on my burgeoning intellect.

I abandoned the pretence of unpacking properly and simply threw everything higgledy-piggledy into drawers, almost revelling in the gratuitous abandonment I'd not been allowed to indulge in at home. I took another look at Peter and braced myself to make another overture of friendship.

'You look like you're working hard already.'

It wasn't the most original thing I could have said and it was more in the way of being a statement than a question, but he obviously felt it couldn't be ignored so it served its purpose.

'I wanted to get a head start. I need to work my socks off if I want to get a good degree.'

His voice was thin and reedy and suited the rest of him. He could have sounded pompous, or as though he had a chip on his shoulder – and I did feel a faint flicker of guilt for being one of those people who could get away with doing little work and still walk away with good results – but he didn't. It had been said as a simple statement of fact and that made me warm to him, just a bit.

'I'm going to head over to the main house,' I said, 'Go and mingle a bit.'

Again, I felt the inadequacy of my own conversation, but he took the implied offer and to my surprise, turned the lamp off and followed me back through the grounds to the building at their centre.

The walk, although brief, provided me with an opportunity to take more notice of my surroundings, as I was no longer preoccupied by a suitcase hovering on the brink of imminent collapse. To my untutored eye, there wasn't much in the gardens to inspire deeper thought and I felt a sudden yearning for home. Devon was pretty enough, I suppose, but it had little to appeal to an adolescent who was a city boy to his core. The rolling landscape held no great attraction to one whose ideal view was the city of London from Tower Bridge: a sprawling cityscape where you were jostled impatiently should you ever have the temerity to attempt a moment to stop and appreciate the sights around you. It was a city impregnated with history but obsessively focused on the immediate; intimately aware of its heritage but insistent on living in the now. London, with its safety net of anonymity, where you could *be* whoever you wanted, *do* whatever you liked and no-one would even give you the satisfaction of a second glance. After all, who were you to warrant one? We've seen it all before, their indifference shouted at you. You were no-one special, just another living dot on a landscape so diverse, it believed itself to be unshockable. It was totally at odds with this area of the country and I felt the difference in my heart with a sudden longing for the hard pavements and grimy air of the capital. The fresh air here was suffocating. The gruff tones and lost letters that belied the caring heart within my home city had been replaced by the softer sounds of the West Country. Its gently modulated tones were accompanied by kind-eyed looks that spoke of a genuine desire to know you better. Gone was the frenetic pace of life that screamed in your ear, telling you that like a child late for a school trip, you'd get left behind if you paused to take a breath and savour the moment. A much calmer, quieter voice took its place, reminding you to look around. It didn't want you to miss the red-orange smoulder of the sunset that illuminated fields full of grazing sheep, the glow of the dying day setting the white wool afire.

It should have made me feel more relaxed, but it didn't. I still felt like that child: I hadn't quite given up hope that something, or someone, would come along and rescue me, but was experiencing the dawning misery that I was the proverbial fish out of water here. This was not my home territory and I would have to fight to keep my standing. I wanted to have my intellect recognised, to prove I deserved to be here. I needed reassurance that being rejected from Cambridge did not signify the end of my dreams – this was the beginning of a new and different, but equally exciting future. My Cambridge failure had left me feeling as though my life had ended before it had even begun. I'd been so focused on the path I'd set out for myself that I failed to anticipate that just occasionally, life cannot be planned. The world doesn't read the script you've written for yourself and its author sometimes decides your character must travel a different path.

In this latter area at least, I knew I would not be alone. During my brief wait in the hall prior to being assigned to my room, I had overheard part of a whispered conversation.

'Of *course* you can do this, sweetheart. Oxford just wasn't meant to be; you're *more* than clever enough to be here.'

'I *am* good enough,' I told myself.

Maybe if I told myself often enough, I would begin to believe it.

These musings occupied me until I became aware that the sharp crunching underfoot had changed to the silence of the tarmac, melted into submission beneath the many feet that had trodden its well-worn surface. This change signalled we had almost reached the back of the house and it drew me out of my funk and focused me back in the present. I turned to Peter with a rueful grin as I pushed the door open and prayed he'd not said anything important while my thoughts had been wandering. As my mum would have no doubt reminded me, had she not already been on her way back eastwards; he may not have been destined to become my best friend, but he'd done nothing to deserve my rudeness, however inadvertent it may have been.

That started me thinking about home once again and I slammed the gate on that particular avenue of thought, not wanting to lose myself for a second time in memories of home. It was tempting to meander down that road, but however comforting those contemplations might have been, I needed to be here, now. The two hundred and fifty miles that separated me from everything I knew could have been a whole world away for all the good that thinking about it would do me. Home was safe and this was scary, but scary was good. Scary got the adrenaline going and kept me on my toes. Scary meant I was pushing the boundaries and making myself a better person. This was a challenge I was ready for, one I fully intended to face head on and overcome. I *would* seek out the people who I'd spend the next year living with, I *would* make friends and I *would* be a success. This was the mantra I repeated to myself through the library and the laundry room, along the corridor and out into the main entrance hall. Earlier, it had been full of freshers, dragging bags and saying their goodbyes to parents, some of whom were embarrassingly tearful. Now it was eerily quiet and gave the impression it was mourning its lost occupants. I spared little thought for its faded grandeur; gave even less thought to how many scenes of grieved departing it had been witness to and considered only how its emptiness reflected the way I felt. I hesitated, immobilised by a nauseating wave of anxiety and it wasn't until Peter stumbled over the raised edge of the rug and knocked into me, that I summoned up the courage to face the door to the Common Room.

I took a deep breath and pushed against the heavy oak fire door, unconsciously rubbing my fingers over the rough surface of the gnarled and knotted wood for good luck, in much the same way I realised, as my mum would have done. The resistance from the door seemed to sympathise with my reluctance to enter the room. It was as though it sensed, in its aged wisdom, my need for those extra few seconds to prepare myself for this initial encounter. Then, suddenly, I was in the middle of the madness.

Names and faces flew at me from every direction, verbal assaults that engulfed me until I barely remembered my own name. I introduced Peter along with myself, knowing instinctively that left to his own devices, he would fade into nothingness. He obviously didn't understand the importance of first meetings and he would be written off before he'd even begun if I didn't help him out. My sense of responsibility towards him was however, at war with the equally pressing desire to not be associated with him, as though his oddness would somehow be transferred to me and we would forever be known as 'the weirdos from Room Three'.

Eventually, the tumult ceased and I found myself ensconced in the middle of a small group of boys, chatting about our respective tastes in music. Peter had drifted somewhere to the periphery of the room and was being shepherded by some of the Year Two and Three students who had chosen to stay in halls for a second year. My companions, it seemed, were housed in the stable block, the only mixed residence and I felt a slight twinge of resentment as already I could tell that this was where most of the fun would be happening. These were my kind of people; all from the South and up for having a laugh while they studied.

It wasn't that I had anything against people from the North, I just hadn't met many of them and those I had come across, had not made a good impression. There was one in particular who stood out in my memory; a fat man from Manchester whom I had encountered when on a family holiday in Majorca. The resort had been all-inclusive and the vast majority of patrons had not taken this to extremes. This man, however, was the exception and I remembered him vividly. The sight of his monkey-like stomach – complete with thick dark hair curling obscenely around itself – protruding over skimpy Union Jack speedos, had imprinted itself indelibly on my seven year old brain. He had marched up to the bar and ordered seven pints of lager, all for himself. The poor, harassed barman tried to explain that the hotel's rules were such that he was not allowed to serve more than four pints to one person, but monstrous Manchester man didn't care.

'If it's all-inclusive I can have as many pints as I want.'

In vain, the barman pointed out that while Sir's assertion was quite correct, he still wasn't allowed more than four in any one trip to the bar. *If, however,* the patient voice continued in a rather weary tone, *Sir would like to take four now, he could come back later for another three, should he still require them.* It took some little time for this maths to penetrate the primordial brain and be confirmed, but eventually, he subsided and waddled back to where his equally corpulent wife sprawled on a sunbed. She was bedecked in a loud floral swimsuit and screeched at him that he was a selfish pig, who had forgotten her Campari and soda. On hearing her voice, my father remarked that he was no longer surprised Manchester Man wanted seven pints.

'I'm only surprised he doesn't need more,' Mum said drily.

Thus far, this had been my main encounter with people from the other end of the country and so it was understandable I think, that I viewed them almost as a breed apart, as somehow 'not quite the same' as the people I knew.

The door to the Common Room opened again and drew

my attention away from an evaluation of Radiohead's latest release. Two girls entered, each forming a striking contrast to the other. The leader was tall and slender, almost to the point of thinness with an angular face, high pointed cheekbones and a dark pixie crop that would have looked boyish on almost anyone else but suited her. She couldn't have been described as pretty, even by her friends, but she was intimidatingly confident, her gaze sweeping over us all, coolly assessing. I got the distinct feeling she was judging who would be worthy of her friendship, should they be lucky enough to have it bestowed upon them. The gaze fell on me and her face took on a calculating gleam that terrified me, before it was instantly masked and replaced by an expression which might have looked friendly, had I not seen the look that preceded it. Instead, it looked predatory.

Juxtaposed, was the girl who stood slightly behind her. Her position, half-hidden behind the ice queen, mirrored their contrasting introductions to the room. Soft waves of blond hair framed a round face that smiled gently, almost asking permission to be liked. Her demeanour was far meeker than her compatriot's, but the way she held her head up and kept her back ramrod straight made me admire her. It was clear she was nervous but had girded herself to go through the ordeal and do it properly. I sympathised with both her feelings and her determination to overcome them. How could I not, when they so closely matched my own? I also admired her. I kept my insecurities tightly locked away, masked by an air of false confidence, whereas she was brave enough to acknowledge them openly.

Her eyes darted around the room just as the dark eyes of the other girl had done, but the blue contemplation was less calculating and more in the way of searching for a friendly face. I felt her gaze fall on me and I gave her an encouraging grin. When I received a tentative one in return, her eyes creasing at the corners with the uplift of her mouth, I felt a jolt of electricity run through me and a current pulsed the length of my body.

Turning slightly, the taller girl murmured something to her and they made their way through the tightly packed chairs to where we sat.

'Hi, I'm Zoe,' dark hair said, dropping languidly into the chair she had pulled up next to mine. 'No umlaut,' she continued, looking directly at me, leaving me wondering if she had somehow divined that German was a major part of my degree and if this was a bizarre attempt at flirtation.

Her friend perched awkwardly on the arm of the chair, as there were no others that weren't already occupied and I had to resist the urge to jump up and offer her mine. Whether this was through a misplaced sense of chivalry however, or merely a desire to remove myself from the proximity of Zoe's intimidating presence and strong perfume, I wasn't entirely sure.

'I'm Olivia,' she introduced herself, 'but everyone calls me Livvy.'

Her smile was bright, but her eyes retained their anxious look and I knew, even then, that she would always be 'Olivia' to me. I didn't want to be everyone to her. I wanted to be everything. Until this point in my life girls were something I'd only been hypothetically interested in and I didn't have the words to describe how I felt. There was one, but it was ridiculous to even think of using it. I barely knew the girl, for heaven's sake! How could I even consider using that word? All I knew for certain was that I would willingly endure Zoe's overblown overtures if it meant that I could be in close proximity to Olivia, who turned out to be Zoe's roommate.

Everyone knows the stories of Robin Hood and King Arthur.
Everyone knows they're just legends.

But what if everyone is wrong?

While Sam, Henry and Arthur think they're going to spend their summer holiday with Uncle Alan, their adventurous relative has other plans. The silver arrow has gone missing, and Robin has been kidnapped.

The race is on to find the arrow and rescue Robin, before others beat them to it. Who can be trusted? One wrong move and disaster is sure to follow!

Seven Years Earlier...

The woman stopped at the edge of the road. The streetlights had gone out. Darkness shrouded everything. Two faint pinpricks of light in the far distance provided the only illumination. The hedges lining the borders of the gardens behind her were almost invisible, their edges blurred and smudged into the night. She wondered, not for the first time, if she was doing the right thing. But what other choice did she have? He would never stop looking for her and she had other priorities now. Her hiding place was no longer safe – he was growing ever more powerful, and he would find her eventually. There was only one person she could turn to. One place he would never think to look for her. It was a risk, but what other choice did she have? She had to get away.

Tears chilled her cheeks, but she brushed them away. She couldn't think about her husband, or she'd lose her remaining courage. He was a good man who didn't deserve this, but that couldn't be helped. One day perhaps, he would understand.

Wrapping her arms around her middle, she whispered a few words of encouragement to herself. 'The spell will work. The spell will work.' She had to believe it. The alternative was impossible to consider.

The lights were bigger now. Closer.

Muttering the words of the spell under her breath, she closed her eyes and stepped off the kerb. There was a screech of grinding metal and a smell of burnt rubber hung in the air, clinging to the droplets of rain that caressed the pale skin, turning the red stream pink.

When the driver emerged from the vehicle, he looked at the broken body, its blonde hair bright against the dark tarmac and smiled. Returning to the car, he reversed and pulled away into the darkness, satisfied with his night's work. As the car's taillights were swallowed up by the shadows, the road behind lay empty.

Chapter One

The summer holiday stretched out in front of him with promises of lazy mornings and no alarm clocks. Long, bright days with nothing to do. Exams over, for one glorious summer, he could go out for a run, read books solely for pleasure and play on his PlayStation without feeling the nagging guilt that he should be studying. Fifteen-year-old Sam Huntingdon stretched out in his bed, his pose mirroring that of the cat lying across his feet. He stared at the shapes the cracks made in the ceiling and revelled in the fact it was Monday morning, and he didn't have to get up for school.

Through the floor he could hear his family moving around, getting ready for the day ahead; the clink of spoons on cereal bowls, the metallic pop of the toaster and his youngest brother's muffled voice as he chattered excitedly about nothing in particular. A door banged somewhere, the tremor in the walls reverberating through the house. It was shortly followed by a familiar thudding on the stairs. Sam counted to five in his head and grimaced as his bedroom door flew open. It bounced off the wall behind it to reveal a slightly built boy with a shock of blond hair that stuck up from the crown of his head, giving him the permanent appearance of having just rolled out of bed.

'You need a haircut.' Sam pulled the duvet back over his head.

'I always need a haircut. Mum says there's no point 'cos it still sticks up.' His brother clambered cheerfully onto the bed and sat on him, pulling the duvet away from his face. 'Anyway,' he continued, ignoring Sam's growled comments about annoying little brothers, 'Yours is the same.'

'The difference is, Henry, mine's meant to look like that. It's called a hairstyle.'

'I didn't know a chicken's head was a hairstyle!' Henry flashed his brother a cheeky grin and then ducked as Sam made a half-hearted swing at him.

Knowing it would now be futile to make any further attempts to sleep, Sam swung his legs out of bed and good-naturedly ruffled his brother's hair, then wrapped his dressing gown tightly around himself.

'What did you want anyway, short stuff? Or did you come up here with the sole purpose of stopping me enjoying the first lie in of the holidays?'

'Don't complain – you've been off for weeks while some of us have still had to go to school.'

'That was called study leave, Henry. And even when my exams were over, I still had to get up because Arthur wanted me to take him to school. I'll ask again. Why are you up here?'

'Mum sent me to get you up. Uncle Alan rang this morning to ask if we'd like to go and stay with him for a couple of weeks. He said he'd take us to the Robin Hood Festival.'

Sam rolled his eyes. Henry had been obsessed with the legend of Robin Hood ever since they'd gone on a day trip to the festival two years earlier. He'd persuaded their mother to buy him the green hat and a toy bow and arrow and had worn them for the rest of the summer. Keen to encourage Henry to read more, she'd also bought him two books about Robin Hood. Eventually, Henry memorised most of the tales and began creating his own versions of them, with their youngest brother, Arthur, taking different roles as required. Occasionally, Sam himself was roped in to be the villainous Guy of Gisburne, invariably losing to the heroic Robin. According to

Henry, Alan – already awarded the title of honorary uncle in spite of his being no blood relation – had been upgraded to the status of legend when they'd discovered he had a small tattoo of the silver arrow on his wrist. It had always been concealed beneath his watch, but Henry had spotted it one day when they'd been out for a walk.

'That's awesome! When did you get it?'

Alan had glanced at his wrist and pulled his watch back over it, as though embarrassed they'd seen it.

'A long time ago. I'd almost forgotten about it.'

'It's seriously cool.'

Sam smiled at the memory. Henry had spent weeks begging their parents to let him get a similar tattoo.

'Did Alan say anything else?'

Henry shook his head. 'Not really. Mum's phoning Dad now to see what he thinks about us going.'

Jumping off the bed, Henry ran back downstairs, leaving Sam to follow more slowly. On reaching the bottom step, he could hear their mother on the phone.

'No, of course I didn't. He rang me! Alan insisted he was happy to have all three of them. If you want my opinion, he's a bit lonely. You know what he's been like since Lily died, and over the summer he doesn't have work as a distraction.' There was a brief silence, then she continued. 'No, me neither.'

Sam paused. Alan's wife, Lily had gone out one night and never returned. The police had searched everywhere, but in the end concluded she was most likely dead. Her body had never been found and, at first, the police had viewed Alan as the main suspect, as he'd been unable to provide an alibi. Henry and Arthur were both too young to remember her, but Sam had been in primary school at the time, and he remembered how devastated his uncle had been. Alan still refused to speak about it, even to Sam's mum and dad, who were his best friends.

Alan had met Sam's mum when they started their first teaching job together. Over several drinks and extensive chats about the difficulties faced by first year teachers, they'd become friends. Even after Alan and Lily had moved to the little cottage in Edwinstowe and the Huntingdons had moved to London, the two families remained close.

Sam entered the kitchen as his mum ended the call. She turned to greet him, a bright smile on her face.

'I take it Henry told you about Alan's offer?'

'Mmm.' Sam nodded, taking a bite out of the piece of toast he'd just picked up.

'Hey!' His mother swatted his hand away affectionately. 'That was for your brother.'

Sam shrugged. 'He'll live.'

Taking another piece of bread out of the packet on the kitchen top, he slotted it into the toaster. His phone buzzed in his pocket. A few seconds later it buzzed again and then a third time. His mother raised her eyebrows.

'Aren't you going to answer?'

He rolled his eyes. 'It's too early for a row.'

She changed the subject. 'Do you want to go to Alan's?'

'Don't mind. They will though.' He nodded towards the living room where he could hear his brothers arguing over who should have control of the television remote.

'What about Philippa? You okay about not seeing her for a couple of weeks?'

'She'll be working most of the summer anyway and then she's going to Greece with her family. We wouldn't have seen much of each other anyway.'

She looked at him with narrowed eyes, but he pretended to be watching the bread in the toaster. Things hadn't been great between him and his girlfriend recently, but he didn't want to talk to his mum about it. Not yet.

'When do we go?' He took another bite of the toast.

'Two weeks today. We'll put you on the train at St. Pancras and Alan said he'd meet you at the other end. Do you think you'll be able to manage with the bags and those two?' She nodded her head towards the living room. Arthur was watching *Scooby Doo*, the remote wedged under his leg, while Henry jabbed him with a cereal spoon.

Sam nodded, his mouth still full of the pilfered toast. He swallowed.

'They'll be fine. Give them a games console and a book each and I won't hear a sound out of them all journey. Don't worry, we'll survive without you.'

'It's not you I'm worried about! Mind you, Alan knows what he's letting himself in for. You've stayed with him often enough before and he knows what you three are like. You will behave though, won't you?'

Sam rolled his eyes again.

'I mean it, Sam. I know they can be annoying, but you're not always the most patient with them and they don't react well to you ordering them around.'

'I'll try. Alan will be there anyway and they're always good for him.' His mum gave him a stern look. 'He said I could drop the 'uncle' when I got to sixteen.' Sam said defensively. 'My birthday's only a few weeks away.'

The toast popped and she smothered it in honey before giving it to Sam to carry into the living room.

'Give that to Arthur, will you, love? And tell him to be careful with it. You know what a mess he can make.'

Sam passed the warning on to his youngest brother and sat down next to him, glad of the excuse to watch TV. He stole the remote from under his brother's leg but left it on the same channel. *You're never too old for Scooby Doo.*

'Folly'

1917

Avonstow is at war, but it's a friendly invasion that forces deeply held secrets to emerge. The arrival of the Australian engineers upsets the equilibrium of the wartime village, while the commander of the village's naval base is convinced a spy is lurking in their midst. The consequences are far greater than anyone might have imagined.

1995

Ellie Whitemore travels to Avonstow after her great-uncle's body is discovered on the salt marshes near the town. She sets about unravelling her family's past and finds that their fortunes are inextricably linked with those of the town itself. But there is always a price to pay when secrets are unearthed.

January 1904

Excited screams bounced off the trees surrounding the frozen pond. It sounded as though every child in Avonstow had gathered with the sole purpose of making as much noise as possible.

John stood to one side. Alone. Uncertain. Invisible. The outsider. He'd grown up in the village just the same as the others, but he wasn't one of them. He had an Irish father. He shivered.

Snatches of conversation drifted across the ice, carried on the chill wind.

Go on... no, you do it... He won't do it... too scared... Coward... Fenian...

John closed his eyes, trying to block them out. One moment his woolly hat was jammed over his eyebrows, the next, he felt it snatched off. He opened his eyes to see it lying in the middle of the ice.

Da's going to murder me. That was a present from Maimeó.

'Where's your hat, Liversidge? You just gonna leave it there?'

The speaker was a short, stocky boy, the leader of the gang who made John's life miserable.

'Oh, leave him be, Arnie.' Seven-year-old Alice Thompson was trying to be nice, but her kindness only made John feel worse.

Letting a girl fight your battles now? You're a miserable little coward. He's half your size and you let him push you around. His father's voice boomed inside John's head.

Slowly, John pushed away from the tree and walked tentatively towards the edge of the pond. He put a cautious foot on it. It creaked ominously but held his weight.

'Don't be an idiot.' Alice's older brother, Laurence, put a hand on John's shoulder. John shrugged him off and took a second step towards the hat. Then a third. And a fourth. Step by step he reached the centre of the pond, bent to pick up the hat and waved it. Alice stood at the edge of the pond chewing her bottom lip. She wasn't even looking at him. John's triumphant smile faded a little.

Below the cheers, a loud crack went unheard. John felt the ice shift beneath him and he plunged into the freezing water. Cheers turned to screams as pain stabbed at every part of his body.

'Go to The Curry and get his dad!' Alice shouted. Her friend, Lily, tore off in the direction of the pub.

Alice lay on her front and slowly inched her way across the ice. As soon as she was close enough, she stretched out an arm.

'John! Take my hand. You need to pull yourself out. I'm not strong enough.'

Teeth chattering, John did as she instructed. She shouted encouragement at him, and his numbed fingers clawed at the ice, trying to get a firm grip on something. Anything. Several times her hand closed around his wrist, only for him to slide out of her grasp. Alice simply leant further across the pond, still shouting instructions, clutching at his flailing hands.

Eventually, he managed to heave his exhausted body onto the ice beside her.

'Come on! Don't just lay there.'

Alice slithered back across the ice, John copying her actions. As they reached firmer ground, hands pulled him to his feet. Arnie. The younger boy looked terrified. Alice looked between the two of them, then put a small hand on John's arm.

'Please don't tell on him. His dad'll whelp him if he finds out.'

Garrett Liversidge arrived, red-faced and out of breath. He cuffed John around the head.

'What the devil were you playing at?'

John didn't reply. Keeping his head down he stared at the hat clenched in his hand.

'He's okay, Mr. Liversidge,' Alice said. 'It was an accident.'

'Is that right, now?'

John nodded. 'We were playing at the edge. I took my hat off because I was hot, and it got kicked out there by accident. Arnie was going to get it back, but I said I'd do it myself.'

John didn't miss the black look his father shot at him. He'd be for it when they got home. Alice was the kind of child his father wanted. Someone who took charge. Someone who was strong. Instead, his father regularly raged, he'd been saddled with a snivelling brat who cried himself to sleep every night.

John's father looked at Alice. 'Was it you pulled him out?'

Alice shook her head. 'He got himself out. I just helped a bit.'

Garrett looked surprised but pleased and he clapped a hand on John's shoulder.

'Well done, lad.'

John looked at Alice with renewed admiration, realising in that moment that she had given him a priceless gift. One he couldn't afford to let go. He stepped towards her, out of his father's hearing.

'Thank you for not telling on Arnie,' she whispered.

'Thank you for saving me,' he whispered back. He took her hand and squeezed it tightly. 'I'm going to marry you.'

Alice giggled nervously and colour flushed her pale cheeks. The sight of it almost made John forget how cold he was. He clamped his teeth together to stop them chattering and moved to stand in front of Arnie. He stuck out a hand and Arnie took it cautiously.

'Thanks for helping,' John said loudly. Then he tugged Arnie closer, his face hardening. He lowered his voice. 'You owe me now. There's going to be a few changes in this village.'

John walked alongside his father. He was freezing, but he felt good. Life was going to be different from now on. Arnie was his, as was Alice. His father was going to be so proud.

July 1966

The man stared at the corner of the room. The figure was there again. It never spoke, simply stood and watched. The man wanted to confront it, to ask what it wanted. But there was no point. The man knew exactly why the figure was there. They both knew what he had done. What he'd taken away from the one who now haunted his every waking moment.

'How do I make amends?' he whispered, almost to himself. 'What can I do now, after so long?'

He'd loved her so much. Everything he'd done had been for her. She was the one constant in his life. He saw her everywhere, even now. Every voice was hers. Every smile. Every laugh. But she was always across a street, around a corner, always just out of reach.

Where was she now? Adam would know. Adam always knew everything. It was Adam who reminded him when he forgot things. Adam who was always so cross when he talked about the past. He didn't want to talk to Adam. He shouted too much.

A name came to him and he frowned. That was her name. He loved the sound of it in his head, but it wasn't the one he was looking for. It was the other one he wanted. If only he could remember what it was. Suddenly it came to him and with a trembling hand he wrote it down before he could forget it.

A nurse appeared in front of him and placed a cup of tea on the table. He reached out and closed his fingers around her wrist, pushing the paper towards her with his other hand.

'I want to see her,' he whispered.

The nurse looked at the name on the paper and frowned. 'I'll have to check with your son,' she said.

'No!'

She tried to pull her hand away. Alarmed, he clung onto it.

'No!' he shouted. 'I don't want him. I want her.'

The nurse's eyes widened and she patted his hand reassuringly.

'Very well if that's what you want,' she soothed. 'We'll see what we can manage.'

He laid back against the pillow, suddenly exhausted. He'd loved her beyond reason, but by the time he'd realised his mistake, she'd gone. He'd been blinded by grief and anger. He wanted to punish everyone. What had it all been for though? He'd searched for her, but it was as if she'd become invisible until years later when his father revealed he'd known all along where she was. In that moment he'd hated the old man more than he'd ever thought possible, but at least it had given him the chance to make amends. She would never know what he'd done for her, but he knew and that had to be enough.

Other faces floated into view. Younger ones this time. Not her, but close enough to make his heart ache. He didn't want to think about that time though. He let his mind drift further back. She would come soon. She had to.

-

<u>January 1995</u>

The mud bubbled as the body forced its way to the surface, the once shiny buttons of its uniform now dulled with age. The rust-coloured stain on the khaki fabric told its own tale; a tale of jealousy, of anger, of fear, but mostly a tale of love. In its pockets it still had the note. Her note.

For years the body had lain trapped by the cloying grip of the East Anglian clay, but no more. The tidal surge – the like of which had not been seen since the middle of the century – had wrested it from the embrace of the earth and thrust it to the surface. The relentless power of the sea was unforgiving, and the mud had finally been forced to relinquish that which it had held for so long. The battered coastline and the half-drowned town beyond it bore testament to the force with which the sea had attacked. A more sympathetic onlooker might have considered the residents already had enough to deal with, without the added complications of a flood and a corpse. But the body was past caring about others. It had waited long enough. Now it was free. Now, its face was exposed to the sun again. Now, its story could be told.

Printed in Great Britain
by Amazon